Captive Mafia Wife

A DARK MAFIA ROMANCE

SHANNA HANDEL

Captive Mafia Wife: A Dark Mafia Romance

Twisted Mafia Kings

Shanna Handel

Copyright © 2024 Shanna Handel

All rights reserved.

My marriage is arranged without my consent.

To a distillery owner of the mafia.
Tall, dark, handsome, and...stuffy.
Rich, cocky, and a god with his fingers.
Although dressed impeccably, I can't tolerate him.

He sends his circus man to drag me to his castle.

He makes me wear a stunning wedding dress.
He puts his tongue between my virgin thighs.
Handcuffs me, teases me, makes me beg.
My body wants more; my lawyer brain says run.

He's wrong for me in every way, so why am I addicted to the chase?

THE LUVELY Lass o' Inverness,

Nae joy nor pleasure can she see;

For, e'en and morn she cries, Alas!

And aye the saut tear blin's her e'e.

-Robert Burns

Chapter One

THE DAY FREYA IS TAKEN TO FREDRICK'S ESTATE

F redrick

WITH MY UNWILLING BRIDE-TO-BE ARRIVING IN mere hours, I must focus my energies. To say Freya Burnes will be a challenge is an understatement. For the arrival of this ice-blonde modern-day Valkyrie princess?

I should be armed.

My naked ass is freezing as I plunge my body into the depths of the river's icy waters. The crystal-clear waters pour down from the mountains into the freshwater Loch Ness and out to the sea. Hence, the state of my balls, currently shrinking into my stomach as I breathe through the frigid temperatures. Swimming strengthens every muscle, which I consider a bonus; I swim to sharpen my mind.

My arms slice through the water, and I turn my head, catching a breath and a glimpse of my new home.

I've certainly upgraded from the oak barrel-scented apartment above my Glasgow distillery. I'm now the proud owner of a castle. It's a small one on the scale of medieval architecture for royalty, but a castle all the same. Modeled after the real castle of Inverness, ours is adoringly named Wee Inverness. The red sandstone structure sits on the tall cliff above me, overlooking the full moon of my ass cheeks as I glide through the river.

When Callum recruited me to help protect his sister, I knew I had to isolate beautiful party girl Freya from Glasgow. I lied to myself as I signed my name on the deed to the little castle, closing the cash purchase. I told myself that whoever married her could move here.

Indeed, I wasn't buying it with *me* in mind to be her new husband.

But then, Callum picked me, and who was I to say no to my brother-in-arms? The fact that I would lay down my life to stop a paper from slicing the tip of Freya's perfect finger made me the man her brother chose as her betrothed, revealed in that desperate call he made to me.

Hence, my recent move to Inverness in the thrumming heart of Scotland's lively Highlands.

I knew she'd be kicking and screaming all the way. But she has a deep love of beautiful buildings. Did I buy this castle as a way to bribe my unwilling, captive wife into not trying to scratch my eyes out each time I enter a room?

Absolutely, I did.

I quickly correct myself; I bought the estate knowing Freya, with her love of older homes and grand renovations, couldn't *not* fall in love with it, no matter which man was to bring her here.

"Be honest with yourself, Fredrick." My body finally warm, I dolphin flip, head back toward home, and admit the truth. To say I was obsessed with her the moment I saw her sounds...dramatic. If there's one thing I can't tolerate, it's drama. There's a light in Freya that shines so brightly she blinds me.

I have to have her.

Breathless, I flatten my palms against the stone wall, pushing myself up and out of the water. I'm drawn from my thoughts by a tsk tsk from my house manager, Morvan, who stands at the edge of the waters, her new blue-emblemed apron tied around her waist, an oversized towel draped over one arm.

When I first met her, she told me her Scottish name is pronounced *MAWR-vein,* which means "big mountain. " She also told me she came with the wee castle, daring me to try to fire her.

I declined the dare, doubled her salary, and moved her from the tiny garden shed, which had been converted to a one-bedroom, one-bathroom apartment, to a larger guest house with a small kitchen and a soaker tub to ease her back at the end of a long day of work.

I offered to house her husband as well. She declined. I didn't pry.

I've taken to calling her MAWR-vein in my head.

She's a tiny, round person. Her namesake is in her determination, not her stature.

"Mr. Fredrick, you're going to corrupt the young ladies in the town. I beg you—cover up this instant." She hands me the towel.

I thank her and am grateful for the soft warmth wrapping it around my waist. "Not much to corrupt them with after that ice-cold swim."

"Gah! You're terrible! Dry off and get dressed. I have a fire and fresh coffee waiting for you in the kitchen. Haste ye back! Five minutes."

"Yes, Morven," I call to her, but she's already making her way up the grassy hill, chastising me under her breath as she goes.

After dressing, more chastising about how I'll catch my death of cold or get eaten by a monster in that river, and two cups of hot black coffee, I move about my home, awaiting my bride. With her stunning beauty, impeccable manners, and quick wit, she was born to host in this house. Her brilliant mind and nerves of steel round her out, making her a wife any mafia man would covet.

I'm the only one who can rein her in to keep her safe. As stubborn as she is strong, Freya has a wild streak in her burning brightly, suiting her family name.

But she can't burn me. One look in her glass-green eyes and I knew I could tame the soaring flames of the raging bonfire that burns within her. Not dim them or snuff her fire out as other men might...

Instead, banking them to a soft flame that lights a candlewick. From daring fire to gentle flicker. I'll give her the world in return. Freya loves fine homes, stunning jewelry, custom clothing, and fast cars. She'll have it all.

A staff member comes to tell me she's arrived. I find myself doing a slow jog down the stone steps that lead to the pebbled drive. I glance down at my watch. "Anytime now." I start to pace as I wait, then stop myself.

She's like a big cat; any sign of weakness, she'll pounce.

Instead, I glance down, studying my dark gray suit jacket, searching for lint. As always, thanks to MAWR-vein, I'm spotless. My eyes focus on the road, and I fiddle with my cuff links. I slide my hands in my pockets.

Freya has arrived.

She steps out of the sleek black car I sent for her. Typically, she wears all-black, classic couture, head to toe. Today is the same; her sleek black dress is elegance personified. But something is different about her. Her long, white-blonde hair is swept up in a tight updo, and a black lace veil is perched on top of her head.

Standing behind the open door of the black car, she takes in the estate from behind dark, massive, cat-eyed Chanel sunglasses. Striding on those long pale legs atop black heels as thin as pencils, she moves around the door, allowing the driver to close it behind her.

Her gaze finds me. I can feel her staring at me from behind those glasses. I stare back as she makes a point of striking a pose, jutting out a defiant hip. She raises her black, lacquered fingernails to the top of her head.

And flips a swath of black lace over her face.

I can't help the smirk that tugs at the corner of my mouth. Her feisty spirit is part of what draws me to her. Now, she's come, dressed...for a funeral.

"You may have brought me here as your captive," she says as she breezes past me. "But there will be no wedding."

I slip in front of her, stopping her movement forward. An immovable wall of a man just as determined as herself. She's finally met her match.

"There will most certainly be a wedding."

"Look, Freddie. Callum's worried, and it's not a good look on him. I've never seen him anything other than cocksure of himself. So, I'm here. I'll let you play out your fairy tale, pull a Rapunzel, and lock me away in a tower for safekeeping. Or heck, be the Beast if you want, but we"—she points from me to her, then back to me—"will never, ever be married." She looks to the sky. "Pray for me, my sweet island!"

Shaking it off, I ignore her prayers. "I disagree."

I grip the delicate lace between my fingers, slowly lifting the veil and folding it over the barrette that pins it in her hair. Gently taking hold of the arms of her sunglasses, I slip them from her beautiful face. "And what I say goes."

Her eyes, green like her brother's, focus on the light. She studies my face. Clouds roll through her sparkling gaze. "You're not the only one used to getting their way."

"No, I'm not. But I am responsible for you and your safety. And the best way to keep you safe? Make you my wife."

Her head cocks to the side. "Neither of us will be safe if you try and force me to marry you because then I'd have to kill you."

"Is that so?"

"'Tis so, I'm afraid," she sighs. "I don't take kindly to demands involving the words, 'till death do us part.'"

"But then I'd be dead and you'd be in prison," I state.

"Aye, and only the best lawyer—" She raises her brows at me. "That would be me—would be able to keep me out of prison."

With that, she snatches her glasses from my fingers, settles them back on her face, and blows me a kiss as she glides past me, stomping her heels up the stone steps to her new home.

She's a perfect picture—she could be a painting, Parisian artwork hanging over my mantle. Her dress is tailored to her slim frame, the black lace against her immaculately styled fair hair, perfectly silhouetted against the grassy hills behind her as she pauses on the stone-pebbled walk before the red stone castle, looking to her left, taking in the view of the river, sparkling under the sunlight.

My heart lodges in my throat. Thick with desire, I swallow down the lump, quietly chastising myself. "Patience, Fredrick. Patience."

I'll give her things money can't buy. Kindness, trust, respect, the list goes on. Together, we will forge a new empire.

And she will have it all.

Except for the one thing I won't give her. Something so dangerous that it has no place in our brave new world.

Love.

You can't give what you don't have.

Chapter Two

A FEW WEEKS EARLIER, ON ALL HALLOWS EVE...

Freya

MY FRENEMY PATRICK PATERSON RUNS A HAND over his square jaw as he eyes my client. "So, you're telling me that on the night in question, the one where you *claim* your boyfriend attempted to accost you, you had on...a *red* dress? One that the jury can clearly see resembles a nightgown more than an outfit. Wouldn't a woman wear a dress like that in order to seduce her man, to make him—"

"My Lord, surely my learned colleague is not implying something derogatory about my client!" I'm seething. It's the old boys' club's defense, placing a female victim at fault for her own murder or assault because her skirt was too short. I know Patrick isn't this backward of a thinker; he's a staunch feminist, but he'll do anything to win.

Raised an islander, I'm not willing to compromise my

morals. My values enter those imposing courtroom doors with me and stick. I will win.

I pop up from my chair and flip my icy blonde hair over my shoulder to prove my point. "My client's outfit has nothing to do with this case. Surely, we have evolved from the days when we judge someone's character by their looks. Or their clothing." I shift my weight, bringing attention to the stilettos I wear. "I love fashion. It doesn't make me a dummy. I had to work my ass—"

"Language, Ms. Burnes."

"I apologize, my Lord. I meant that I've worked hard to become successful enough to purchase this black Gucci suit I wear." There are six women on the twelve-member jury in this civil case. I eye them all. "And it looks good, right?"

I get a few nods and smiles from the more progressive women. And poison darts from two others, clutching their pearls as they shake their heads at my red-soled shoes and the fact that I wear nothing underneath the buttoned suit jacket.

"My Lord, may I say, I don't dress like this for any man." I stress my point while trying to invalidate Patrick's. "I do it for myself. Because I like how I look. I feel good. I feel like myself, my Lord. But in doing so, I am not inviting assault. Grown adults should be able to exercise self-control."

The white-haired judge gives a heavy sigh. "Yes, I believe you are most likely correct, Ms. Burnes. Let us move on, Mr. Paterson."

"Thank you, my Lord." I hide the victorious smile that lights up my insides.

Patrick moves on. I sink back down in my seat. The judges are all starting to get used to me. The male lawyers know me by now; dare I say, they've stopped admiring my calves openly.

On the floor of the courtroom, they're starting to fear me.

Later, when we're done for the day, I sail past Patrick, pulling my coat tighter around me in the fall breeze, eager to get home and change into my costume. Pretty autumn leaves swirl around us.

He reaches out, snapping a leaf up between a finger and thumb. He hands it to me. "For you, my dear."

"Thanks." I take the pretty leaf, twirling it between my fingers. Red with gold tips. Once we step into the fresh air and onto the concrete steps at the front of the courthouse, we're no longer enemies. The solicitor crowd in Glasgow is close—brutal warriors by day, partners in partying by night. "You're still coming tonight? Even though I kicked your ass in there?"

He raises his brows jokingly. "Isn't All Hallows Eve a night for prayer and fasting?"

"Nope," I say. "Drinking and debauchery."

"Freya, Freya, Freya. You're going to be the death of me." He gives a deep groan and rolls his eyes. "Of course, I'll be there. I would never miss the Annual Burnes Bash. I'll be the cowboy in the black leather chaps for your Samhain party."

I wince at his words. Samhain is what we Scots call Halloween, but I find All Hallows Eve so much more spectacular for the name of the most important night of the year.

I let it slide.

"Yeehaw, hawt cowboy!" I stretch upward, pecking a platonic farewell kiss on his cheek. "See you tonight!"

Home again, I dive into costume preparations, my sister-in-law Fiona and I talking animatedly as I do our collective makeup. She hurries off to change, and I quickly dress. Time is ticking by, and guests will be here soon.

Fully ready in ten minutes, I strut down the hall like it's a London catwalk. "I am feeling myself in this costume!"

At the top of our double spiral staircase, I lean down to check my reflection in the spiderweb-covered mirror. This year, I'm wearing a black, long-sleeved dress with the word PURPLE written down the center of my body. Three white lines stretch across both my collarbone and kneecaps, and calf leather, soft-as-velvet knee-high boots streamline the black casing of my marker costume.

My bright purple wig tilts on my head, and I reach up to straighten it.

"Perfect in purple." I give myself a nod.

My brother's deep voice fills the landing. "What are you supposed to be? A crayon?"

Embarrassed to be caught checking my costume—again—I stiffen. "I'm a marker. See?" I point at the letters running down my front. "All black plastic with the name of the color in white, with purple at the top." I point to purple Sasha. "Where the felt-tip marker thingy is."

He's got something in the hollow of one palm. On closer look, I see the candied pecans I made for the party. Correction, requested Cheffie to make. I'm not allowed near the stove after an incident involving me, a fire, and a frozen pizza.

He pops one in his mouth. He shrugs. "Same as a crayon."

"Callum Burnes, you are infuriating." I start ticking off on my fingers. "A—I told you not to touch the food till the guests arrive." Callum and his massive men casually grazing a table of snacks can hoover the entire spread in a matter of minutes. "And B—crayons are all one color, AND they don't write the name of the color on the crayon, just the brand."

"Yes, they do," he says.

Hands to my hips, I say, "No, they don't."

"They do." Intent on raising my blood pressure to stroke levels, he crunches on another pecan before saying, "I remember asking Miss Jane what the hell 'burnt sienna' was and getting a demerit for language."

"Let's agree to disagree—we're likely both wrong. And you only remember Miss Jane's class because you had a crush on her. When she was like forty, and you were nine. Gross."

He gives me that cocksure smile of his. "What can I say? I'm an early bloomer?"

"Ha!" I challenge. "Not in monogamy. That's fairly new to you."

"Fiona is the only woman who could tame my Viking blood." He finishes his illegal snacking and brushes his hands off. His grin drops, his bottle-green gaze going severe. "Speaking of, when will we be getting you married off?"

"Let me see." I bring my wrist up to glance down at my nonexistent watch. "How about half past NEVER?"

Tired of the subject, I step from the landing to the top of the stairs, but Callum grabs my arm. "Freya." He's pulling me back.

"Yes?"

The look on his face makes the tiny, baby-fine hairs on the back of my neck stand on end. "I'm serious," he says.

"Callum. We've discussed this." Like, a thousand times. "I don't need a man to keep me safe."

"Freya, we're not your average family. I keep you as safe as I can, but with Fiona to look after now, I'm terrified I'll miss something and let something slip." Is that a sheen of tears in my brother's gaze? I've only seen him tear up once, on his wedding day. "I'd never forgive myself if anything happened to you."

I soften my tone. "I love you, Callum. And I don't need you to protect me. We have an entire security team to protect our Glasgow Kings. It's not only up to you."

"I know, and they do protect this house, this family. It's your work that scares me. No matter how hard I try—I can't always get our men inside those courtrooms. You know that."

"My work," I say. "I don't deny it's a weak spot in our security."

We've had this conversation many times, talking ourselves in circles trying to devise a solution. But I can't give up law. Without Solicitor Freya, I wouldn't know who I am or who I'd be."

"I want you married. I want a man to protect you, care for you—"

"No more. Not tonight. Please," I plead. "It's our party." Every year, I throw this bash to bring the two halves of our lives together: our steadfast island family and boisterous Glasgow friends.

He heaves a sigh. "Aye. I know how much you love Samhain—"

"All Hallows Eve," I correct. "Aye. My love for the holiday runs deeper than the waters of Loch Morar."

"I'll shut my mouth."

"Thank you, Callum. And don't think I don't know your worry comes from a place of love."

He clears his throat. We Burnes don't do emotions—conversation over. "Drink?" I ask, knowing we can agree on whisky.

"Yeah. I'm going to see if Fiona is ready. I'll meet you at the bar in ten."

"Fiona looks adorable. I just finished her whiskers." I head down the stairs, knowing full well that his checking on his wife will lead to the newlyweds being unable to keep their paws off one another, and it will be much more than ten minutes before he makes it to the bar.

No problem, I don't mind drinking alone. And my girls should be arriving early.

Speak of the devil, and she shall appear! As I pass the front door, it flies open, and women from the firm pile in. They've come early to share a "quiet" drink with me before the party really kicks into gear.

The women are a flurry of sexy witches, frisky kittens, naughty nurses, and vamped-up vampires. I hug them individually, admiring their gorgeous costumes, then lead them to the Great Hall for a drink. I have everything their skanky little hearts could desire.

We enter the renovated Great Hall through the heavy wooden doors that, after multiple tries, I've finally gotten stained with the perfect shade of warm honey. Our iron sconces hang from the white walls, and the room is aglow with flickering candlelight, casting eerie shadows across the walls adorned with webs and black lace, ghosts and ghouls floating overhead. A fire roars in the massive stone fireplace.

Jack-o'-lanterns grin from every corner, their twisted faces adding a slight eeriness to the decor. The air is thick with the scent of pumpkin spice, warming apple cider, and the burning of vanilla-scented candles, creating the heady atmosphere I was striving for. Nailed it!

Tables are laden with the party's signature drink, whisky bottles, candy corn bowls, and caramel apple platters. Cute bartenders serve us, and after sharing a drink with my girls, I excuse myself to greet the steady stream of guests beginning to arrive.

"Everybody on the island is gonna get tipsy!" I sing what I remember of the American pop song, replacing the word club with island, shaking my hips, whisky dribbling on the front of my black dress as I sip at the cup. "I'm getting more on my clothing than in my mouth." I laugh, bringing the cup to my lips as I attempt another sip. "I think I might be a wee bit wrecked!"

"Go easy, Freya," Fiona warns. "You don't want to get sick."

"Oh, Fiona! Where did you come from!" I eye my wee redheaded sister-in-law.

The petite bundle of rules wears a black, skin-tight, full cheetah-print bodysuit and a pair of cat ears on a hairband. "I've been standing here the whole time, silly. Keeping an eye on you. And your wig." Rising on the balls of her feet, she gives me and my wig—a persona named Sasha—a proper straightening.

"You are adorable, aren't you Fi-bee?" I tap a finger against her cutely painted black nose, a job I did way earlier in the evening before I'd started drinking. "Your whiskers held up beautifully!"

"Thanks to my makeup artist." She holds a delicate flute of champagne in one hand, Champers in the other. The wee ginger kitten hates me and goes everywhere with her, never leaping from her arms.

"Cheers, sister!" I rattle the "filled it myself," overly full glass of whisky against her champagne flute, sloshing liquor everywhere.

"How about switching to water." She puts her glass on a table, her face wrinkling with displeasure as she one-handedly wipes her hand on a napkin. "Or a nice cup of tea. Or cheese and bread to soak up all that alcohol?"

"Drink up. Everybody on this island needs to be tipsy tonight."

Fiona's brow wrinkles. "We're not on the island. We're in Glasgow."

"Shite! You're right. Everybody in the city was getting tipsy. Hey! That sounds even better. Thanks, friend." I give her a few bars of the new lyrics.

She seems less than impressed.

Planting a motherly hand on her hip, she shoots me an "I mean business" look. Her brows go sky high as she looks me over from the toes of my knee-high black high-heeled Saint Laurent boots to purple Sasha resting on the top of my head.

She shakes her head and says, "I think I need to go get Callum."

"Gah! No way. Callum is *noooooo* fun." I reach out a fingertip, bopping her lightly on the tip of her nose again. "I, on the upper hand, am fun. Very"—*bop*—"fun."

"And on the *other* hand...ye might be having just a wee bit too much fun." Fiona murmurs something else about getting my brother to lay eyes on me.

"No thanks, babe." I lean down, planting a smooch on her soft cheek, getting a waft of Chanel. "Oh, you smell good. New perfume?"

Already knowing the answer. My brother bought it for her; even though she married into a bottomless bank account, she'd never spend that kind of money on herself.

"Callum got it for me. I adore it. Wear it every day." She leans in and whispers, "But I could never splurge like that on a tiny bottle of liquid."

"You'll learn. I'll teach you," I promise.

I twirl off with a curtsy and a bow to address my other guests. "Everybody in the city gettin' tipsy." I sashay away, calling, "Everybody in the city—is getting tipsy!"

"Heck, yes, we are!" a familiar voice calls out.

Finally! Someone ready to party on my level. I look over my shoulder as Kitt strolls up, the American girl who found herself on the wee island where I grew up. She's practically family, married into our messy little Scottish mafia world.

"Yeeeeehaw!" Kitt calls, looking adorably American in her cowgirl boots, leather hat, and cut-off shorts. I'll have to find Patrick later and get a pic of the two Wild West costumes together. She laughs, clinking her glass against mine. She holds one of my most prized creations, the Spooksicle—a fruity, frozen vodka drink served in a glass that smokes with dry ice as you consume it.

White puffs of air swirl from the open top of her skull-shaped cup.

"Yeehaw to you too, you crazy American bird!" I hold up my glass now with only a splash of alcohol in it with a cheer.

"Cheers," she says. Lowering her voice, she pulls me in closer. "Hey—I just saw Fiona striding off to find your brother. I think your party is about to be shut down—"

"Hell no. That is *so* not happening," I say, borrowing Kitt's LA tone, then quickly trade it out for my best cowgirl twang. "Ya'll have fun now, you hear!"

Leaving Kitt, I make my way through the tight crowd.

Exiting the hall, I breeze through the kitchen, thanking the caterers yet again for their yummy party food, and slip out the back door.

The temperature has dropped since I made my way home from work this afternoon, and a blast of air cools my face, which is flushed from the drink.

The garden is alive with fall colors. Golden leaves cascade from the trees; carpeting the grass, we've just mowed with swaths of reds, oranges, and yellows. Pumpkin lanterns flicker with an ethereal light, casting eerie shadows that dance across the expanse of the garden. The crisp air carries the faint scent of woodsmoke from the bonfire that crackles merrily by the overturned boat bar.

Callum tried to axe my fire under "safety terms," but I would not let him. Samhain fires strengthen the bond of the community; communal fire on the final day of October says it's the start of winter, so let's make sure we all stay warm together!

Fire and food will keep our bonds strong.

Tables groan under the weight of decadent, savory food and colorful gourds while my costumed guests mingle around the parquet dance floor we've installed for the party. I cross over the parquet, pausing in the center to strike a pose.

I move further into the enchanted garden, holding my empty glass in the air. "Drink up all! All of youse!"

A cheer rises from the crowd.

On my way to the bar, I find a group of my law firm girls dancing with some islanders from home. Happy to see my two worlds mixing, I greet, kiss, and shimmy around the crowd.

Carol Ann, a girl from the island I think of like a younger cousin, stomps her boots to the music, shaking her dark curls; the ends are dyed a bright orange in honor of the holiday. She wears a cape and pulls it around her, swooshing it through the air.

A huge fan of vampire romance novels, Carol Ann smiles at me, revealing pointy teeth. "I *vant* to suck yer blood!"

"Later!" I shout over my shoulder as I pass her, making a beeline for the bar. "Need more whisky first!"

"Good! I like blood with high alcohol content best," Carol Ann shouts back.

I turn back over my shoulder, shooting her a grin. "Got you covered!" I say. She laughs as I sprint away for more booze.

"Oooph!" In haste, I've run smack-dab into a solid wall of heat and muscle—the scent of cedarwood, bonfire, and masculine energy. I look up to find deep brown, serious eyes staring down at me, rays of heat and intrigue in those dark pupils. Focused on me like I'm the only one standing out here.

The gorgeous man standing before me is Fredrick Frisque, one of my brother's mates, the French entrepreneur who opened Frisky Whisky, the new distillery and hotspot of Glasgow nightlife. I can't say he hadn't caught my attention when he breezed in my front door earlier tonight.

Any straight woman with a pair of eyes and a working vagina notices the man.

Six feet plus. Dark hair. Dark eyes. Olive skin. Angled cheekbones glide down in flat planes to meet a chiseled jaw. Tall. Dark. Handsome. And he makes a damn fine whisky, the very drink I'm searching for now.

Smoky and oaky, with a hint of clove. Warms you from the inside. It's so yummy going down.

"'Scuse me, Frisky Freddie." Hearing my terrible nickname for him, Sir Fredrick holds in a groan. "Got to get to that bottle right there." I slip past him, grabbing the whisky from behind the bar.

His hand shoots out, grabbing the neck of the bottle I hold. Rude. He eyes my costume. "What are you? A crayon?" Rude AGAIN. His simple statement makes me rethink my entire costume.

Unwilling to give him an ounce of power, I sniff, indignant. "I happen to be a purple marker. It was my favorite of the marker choices when I was little. Everyone in my class knew that, of the collective supplies stored in the center of our group's table, the purple marker belonged to me. Purple-handled scissors as well."

"But as you said, those were communal items."

"And also, as I said, purple was mine." I glance over at Mr. Too-stoic-to-don-a-costume's classic look: a dark gray suit with a crisp white button-down. Gold cuff links match the gold of the buttons on his suit jacket. "And what are you supposed to be? Where's your costume?"

He glances down at the suit in question. "I'm a... blueberry?"

I eye his sleek physique. He's classically *hawt,* an adjective I borrow from LA Kitt. There's no denying it.

"Not a blueberry, hon." He's anything *but* round and juicy. He's ice-cold, older than me, and slightly bitter. "An elderberry popsicle!"

His brow crinkles like he wants to laugh.

"You're killing my buzz, Freddie. I need to remedy that fact." I tilt my head at the whisky. "Can I get that bottle back, now?"

"I think you've had enough for tonight." He not only holds

the delicious liquor further away but reaches out, smoothly taking my glass from my hand.

"Says who?" I punctuate the question with a hiccup. "Oops!"

A large hand wraps around my empty one. "The owner of the whisky you drink."

I snatch my hand back from his. It was generous to supply my party, but if he thinks he can take my drink...he's got another thing coming!

I've met his type before, thinking he can control a woman in the name of helping her. My brother—whom I adore—is the exact same way. Once he married Fiona, he gave up on trying to overprotect me, smartly re-directing all his father-like protection toward his little wife's way.

I'm not a sweet Strawberry Grass flower like our native Fiona. She was waiting for a strong man to pluck her from the green grass of our rolling hills. Me?

I'm single as a Pringle, and that's how I'll remain.

Black nails glint against my pale skin in the moonlight, starkly contrasting with his gorgeous olive complexion as I reach for the cup. "I'll have that back now, thank you very much."

"Not a chance." Holding his arm out straight, he slowly tips the cup over, letting the last tiny drop of his delicious whisky roll down the side of the glass. His eyes never once leave mine during the slow, painful process.

"Pff! I'm off. I haven't even tried the Spooksicle yet." I dismiss him with a wave of my hand as if it's my idea to switch from whisky to vodka. My bare feet sink into the lawn, cold, damp, and lovely against my skin as I leave him.

Wait.

Am I being rude?

I am the host, after all.

I turn to face his disapproval. "Shall I get you one as well?"

He's gone.

I hover as I glance around to find him.

He's gone, gone. *Gone Girl* gone. I shrug.

He smells like a Persian god, but good riddance.

Chapter Three

F reya

IT'S DARK AND QUIETER HERE AT THE REAR OF THE property, the rich scent of Fiona's jasmine flowers in the air. Raised in fresh air and humble homes, my island family and my dearest friends from childhood are drawn to the garden.

They've traveled hours to be here, some taking an overnight ferry from our wee island to the big city of Glasgow. Callum rents a floor of the Sherwood, a local hotel, year-round, so our revolving door of visitors always has a comfy place to stay.

I greet each person as I pass by, thanking them for making the long trek as I head to the whisky. No one here will stop me from completing my mission.

Fiona's four brothers have fashioned an outdoor bar for the night. Sitting on the grass is an upside-down dingy set on two tree stumps, bottles lining its top. Arran, my childhood friend and first kiss, stands behind the boat-turned-bar, holding a bottle of Frisky Whisky to fill a friend's glass.

His smooth voice takes me back to school rugby matches and sneaking smokes behind the caretakers' shed as he greets me with an easy, "Heya Freya."

"Hey, yourself. So glad you came! I know last time we spoke, you weren't sure about your work schedule."

"You know I wouldn't miss it. I hired a couple of extra hands for the week, though I've been driving them crazy with texts, checking on the cattle."

"Of course you are." Arran always was a caretaker. It's part of his personality. I remember many a night he got me home, helping my drunk ass sneak back in through a bedroom window. "I'd forgotten you'd taken over the Bayne ranch."

I go around the bar to hug him but trip over my feet— whoops—and he catches me in his arms. Righting myself, I peck his cheek and throw an arm casually over his shoulders. He smells like fresh hay, mint, and home.

I eye his whisky. "You got some of that for me?"

He eyes me back, brow furrowing. "You sure, love? You look a wee bit..."

"Blootered, steamin', wrecked?" I slap my palms onto the boat's bottom, making a hollow, echoing sound as I blurt out more Scottish slang words for my inebriated state. "Bladdered? Hammered?"

He gives his big, easy laugh. His good nature is what kept us friends long after we stopped kissing. "Aye. Something like that."

"Or am I sloshed and smashed, ooot yer tree, steamboated?" A fresh song with a great beat comes on over the speaker, and I shake my hips.

"I'd say all of the above. Yer mad wae it!" Grabbing a red plastic party cup—Fiona's rule is no glass in the garden—he pours me a splash of liquor, handing me the drink.

I take the cheap cup and throw him a look. "Can I not be trusted with more?"

Folding his arms over the bottom of the boat, he leans in closer. "Nope! You certainly cannae."

"At least put more than a drop in the cup." I try to seduce him to my will with a dance. Red cup aloft, my hands sway to the beat, opposite my rolling hips.

"I don't know—"

"Seriously? I grew up drinking with your rugby team. You know I can hold my own," I say. "Fill 'er up, lad. Fill 'er up!"

"Aye." His pretty eyes sparkle at me. "I never could say no to ye, could I?"

"Not many people dare to try," I tease.

He takes the cup back, pouring in a bit more. "Here ye go, ye wee hellion." He hands it over. "That'll do ya."

"Thanks." I'd forgotten how blue his eyes are. "So, how have you been?" I put my drink on the bar, giving him my full attention. I catch up on his farming adventures, laughing at his stories. We reminisce about old times. We laugh some more.

Ready to return to bro time, Fiona's brothers begin to close in. I give Arran a quick farewell hug and kiss and grab my cup, making my way to the dance floor.

The first few notes of a goddess's melodic voice—the gorgeous, ginger-haired singer for Florence and the Machine—resound through the night air, and I'm instantly elated.

Swaying in the center of the dance floor, lights shining down on me, Florence's voice serenading me, I take in this perfect moment. Licking my lips in anticipation, I finally bring the cup to my mouth, forgiving the cheap plastic vessel that holds the liquid gold. The moment the white rim touches my bottom lip, it's taken away.

"Hey!" I snap my head over my shoulder to see who's stolen my drink. I stare into Fredrick's determined brown eyes once more. "Are you joking? I'd like that back."

He moves in close. Cedarwood and heat. That deep, resonating voice returns, hovering just over my right ear. "You've had enough."

Anger flashes over me. "I'll say when I've had enough."

He captures my chin between his finger and thumb. So not cool. But…I can't deny the dominance of the power move. My knees feel a little weak.

"Party's over, princess," he says. I shrug out of his grasp as he follows up with, "I'll be taking you to bed now."

"Taking me to bed?" An involuntary wave of heat presses between my thighs at the very idea. I let my eyes drag over his broad chest, wide shoulders, Cartier watch, and cuff links. I reach up to bop him on the nose like Fiona, but his stern vibe makes me think better of it; my hand shrinks back. "Hell shall freeze over before that happens, but I will say Kitt was right; you are HAWT."

Hiccup.

Did I say that out loud?

Fredrick grins.

But it's more than just a smile. That cocksure, dangerous facial gesture tells me he thinks he's in control here. My mind goes to the conversation Callum and I had at the top of the stairs. Did he ask Fredrick to keep an eye on me tonight?

Where is Callum?

Ignoring the whisky-stealing, steadfast elderberry popsicle before me, I glance around the garden. Carol Ann leads a group of her and Fiona's friends from home through the gates, overnight bags hanging from their shoulders as they head toward her guest house slash craft cabin where they'll stay the night.

Arran and the boys from earlier are no longer gathered at the boat bar. They're settled around the bonfire with cups of beer from the keg. Their voices are lowered, and their talk has turned reflective as they watch the flames crackle over the logs.

My party is winding down.

"Excuse me, Freddie. I've got to find my brother."

"Party's. Over." He slips an arm in the crook of mine. "Allow me to escort you to your room. I have something to show you. Something I know you need."

Darn him. He's piqued my interest. "Fine. But you go no further than the door. Understood?"

"Sorry." He shakes his head, then runs a hand through his dark hair, showing off how thick it is. I almost want to reach out and touch it. "That won't work," he says. "You'll want privacy for this."

What could it be that he wants to show me? A tickle dances over the back of my neck, telling me to turn down his offer. But anyone who knows me knows I can't leave a mystery unsolved.

I have to know everything.

"You want to come inside my...*bedroom?*" I gulp.

Callum and I bought this estate a couple of years ago so that he could establish the Kings Mafia in Glasgow and I could experience city life. We only just finished the final renovations before this party. I've thrown myself into establishing my place at a new law firm and restoring this house to its former beauty.

I've not dated...anyone.

There's been no man in my bedroom. It was the same as in my childhood home on the island. If I snuck off with a boy, it was always somewhere else.

And I always keep things from going very far.

I tell myself that's why there's a strange, squishy feeling in my belly. I'm just not accustomed to having a man in my room. But I want to know what secret he's keeping.

I'll treat this as a business meeting. "Okay, but I'm only giving you five minutes."

We've reached the back door. He glances down at me, narrowing his brow. "I'll need at least twenty to unwind it."

Now, I'm inquisitive.

Working with my brother as he does, Fredrick's a frequent guest, so he knows his way around the house. We slip through the kitchen, and he leads me to the rear staircase, away from the prying eyes of lingering guests. We reach my door.

He stands beside me, waiting for me to open it. The small signal is another power grab, forcing me to consent to his visit by turning the knob myself. I would face him in a standoff, waiting to see who breaks first and opens the door, but I want to know what it is he's showing me.

"Let's get this over with, shall we?" I slip into the room, leaving the door partway open. He closes it behind us, the metal clicking as it latches.

Suddenly sober, I stand in the center of the room, unsure what to do with my hands. I leave them hanging at my sides and glance around the room. My guest armchair is covered in the discarded outfits I last tried on, leaving the bed open. I am not inviting him to sit on the bed.

"Nice room," he says, strolling around, taking in the pale blue walls, the chandelier suspended from the tray ceiling, the silver bed frame, and the fluffy feather duvets. I may be nearing thirty, but as an unmarried woman, my conservative upbringing still tugs at my conscience for having a man in my room.

Silly, I know, but we girls were taught to keep our legs crossed and our minds on Jesus. Only now, standing here alone with him in my private space, do I realize the enormity of the energy we're exchanging.

One spark and…kaboom.

I take a shaky step back. I feel entirely out of control.

And that's making me fizzin'. I need to get rid of him. Now.

I take another step back, trying to ignore the unsettling heat he's bringing. "Look, Freddie. I don't know your little surprise, but I don't want you in my room. And as you said downstairs, the party's over." I force myself to make eye contact with him. "You've overstayed your welcome. You need to leave."

He closes in, standing right in front of me. There is only a tiny breath of air between us, charged with electricity. He stares down at me, those brown eyes emanating what I can only describe as a primal hunger.

I should never have made eye contact with him. Some otherworldly, beam-like force glues my gaze to his, making it impossible to look away.

He breaks my gaze only long enough to eye the purple wig, most likely sitting askew atop my head. He reaches up, slipping it off. "Purple's not your color," he says, placing her lovingly to the side.

Only now do I remember the hideous netting I've placed over my hair, a wig cap to keep stray blonde hairs from peeking out. Furious at myself for caring what he thinks about me, I rip the pantyhose-like material from my head and toss it to the floor. My hair is knotted at the base of my neck, and flyaway strands surround my face.

I clasp my hands together, hiding the shaking in my fingers. I'm not happy with the baby-sweet way my voice sounds as I whisper, "Show me what you wanted to show me already. Then be on your way."

"Say please," he croons.

"No, thank you."

"You're going to like it." He cups my face in his hand, brushing his thumb's pad against my parted lips. Tingles dance over my skin as he runs it over my bottom lip, dragging it down into a pout before releasing me. A wicked grin covers his handsome face. "I promise."

I almost faint. I thought he was going to try and kiss me. He's playing with fire and dangerously close to crossing a line with me. One that will have him running out of my room begging for an icepack.

What do I do? Kick him in the groin and out the door? Demand that he stop teasing me, quit playing games, and just come out with whatever this surprise is?

Or do I give in to him, give him what he wants, and...

Just. Say. Please.

It's not that simple.

He'll think he owns me if I give him this tiny concession.

But what if he leaves without showing me the thing? As a lawyer, no, as a woman—Patrick doesn't care about half the gossip I give him—I need to know everything, all the time. Curiosity surely would kill me. Plus, I've never known him to lie. If he says I'll like it, I already know I will.

"What do you say?" he asks.

He's no longer touching me, but I feel him all over me. Those eyes burn into me, daring me to play his game. The part of Freya who is quickly turning traitor to my strong woman persona is wondering what it would have felt like to be kissed by him.

"Fine. I'll play." I match his grin, putting on a smirk of my own. "Pretty, pretty please, with a cherry on top."

My breath stuck in my lungs, I wait, expecting him to take something from his suit jacket or pants pocket. Instead, he drops to one knee. What is he doing?

He slides his hands around my waist, staring up at me then running his hands down the outsides of my thighs. When he reaches the hem of my dress, he pinches the cloth between his forefingers and thumbs.

He's shimmying the soft material up my bare skin, past my knee-high black leather boots, revealing my bare-naked thighs, cool air rushing over my legs as the warmth of my clothing disappears. I have no idea what he's planning, but I'm frozen, curiosity and hot desire swirling in me as I stare down at him.

His light touch weakens my knees, and I'm teetering on the spiky heels of my boots. I grab his shoulders. His face is *right there.* I can feel the heat of his breath on my exposed skin. If he moves that dress up even a tiny bit more...

My voice comes out in that weak baby whisper again, my words shaky. "Wha—what are you doing?"

"Kissing you," he says.

I'm only confused for a moment, and then his fingers brush my skin; my dress is up around my waist, and my entire world is split wide open as I balance myself on my boots. His hot breath caresses my skin as he murmurs something against me, hot kisses caressing me over the see-through lace gusset of my black thong.

Fingers digging into his shoulders, I sway into his kiss. The kissing stops, his mouth gone. My eyes flutter open, looking down at him. He holds my gaze, his fingers hooking into the elastic waistband of my thong. He doesn't look away as he tugs it down my thighs, stopping at the tops of my boots.

Heat and shame flash over my face from wanting this so much, knowing it's the wrong man, wrong room, wrong night.

Despite it all, I find myself parting my legs, making it easier for him to drag the panties down over my boots. I've experienced this scene in films before. I always watched with my breath held as the man wound the rolled elastic down the woman's naked thighs, ready to pleasure her.

I never thought it would be me in that scene.

It feels so sexy, so sultry. I'm Freya, the goddess of beauty and debauchery, and this, THIS, is MY All Hallows Eve, and if he wants to worship at the throne of Freya, who am I to stop him?

So, I step out of my panties, but the elastic gets caught in a heel, my new-found sexual confidence momentarily failing me. But he's so smooth, so experienced, he circles a firm hand around my ankle, over my boot, then gently untangles the black lace.

Sliding them into the inner pocket of his suit jacket.

Before I can protest his theft, he's back where he doesn't belong, hands pushing up my dress, his hot mouth on me. My body says otherwise and insists he's right where he should be.

I run my hands through his hair, feeling the silky strands slip through my fingers, wondering if his excellent hair genetics would pass down to his offspring as I tug gently in response to each flick of his tongue, waves of pleasure cascading through my body.

I'm moaning softly with each new surge of ecstasy.

I can feel myself growing closer and closer to the edge, my breath coming in ragged gasps in my struggle to maintain control. But it is a losing battle, and soon, I can't hold back any longer. My fingers tangle in his hair; it really is as thick and luxurious as it looks.

I've lost all power, all control. He's won. And I don't care. I let go. "Fredrick! Oh, God, Fredrick." Crying out his name.

I come hard against his mouth.

Even though I've climaxed, he gently teases me while he continues to suck and nibble on my sensitive spots. I try to push him away. "I can't take anymore..."

But he refuses my protests, murmuring against me, "Yes, you can."

And he slides his finger inside me.

The aftershocks of pleasure continue to ripple through me, each one more intense than the last as he works his tongue against me, his finger moving in me. I can feel my heartbeat pulsing in my ears and hear the rhythmic sound of my ragged breath.

I lean in closer to him, tugging his hair and pulling him even more firmly against me as he draws a second orgasm from me, this one more powerful than the last.

I stand there, mouth gaping, knees quaking, boots shaking, in disbelief at what's just happened, what I've let him do, what he's done to me, and how my body feels like the warm, delicious center of a gooey cinnamon roll pulled out of the oven moments too soon.

I stare down at him, wondering where things go from here.

Slowly, he pulls my dress down, smoothing it back into place. Stands in front of me.

"My—my panties."

Taking them from his suit jacket, he lays the panties in my open palm.

He brushes a chaste kiss against my cheek, his lips soft, the stubble of his chin rough, the smell of cedarwood mingled with... me. To my shame and pleasure, my intimate scent swirls around us.

He pulls away.

And leaves.

Quietly closing the door behind him.

The panties drop from my hand. My mouth gapes.

What in Scotland's Highland Hills just happened?

I zip down a boot, rip it from my foot, and in my frustrated confusion toss it—lightly—I mean, it's a Saint Laurent after all—at the closed door after him, telling him all I should have said the moment he stepped into this room. "Nyaff! Get out, stay out, and never come back!"

I'm speaking to myself. In an empty room. Every nerve ending in my body is still tingling with pleasure from him. It's infuriating. He's infuriating. I can still smell his intoxicating scent, feel his warm, strong hands on my hips, the hot lash of his tongue flickering between my thighs. The worst part?

I want more.

Chapter Four

F redrick

HER TASTE STILL LINGERS ON MY LIPS, intoxicating and addictive, as I head down the stairs. I thought giving in to my desires would finally satisfy the hunger gnawing at me for so long, but it's only strengthened it.

The way she responded to my touch, the way she moaned and arched her back in ecstasy, it was like a drug coursing through my veins, leaving me craving more. I can't shake the feeling that this is just the beginning, that there is so much more to explore with her and more pleasure to discover between us.

I head for the door, ready to call my driver. It's been a night. As I'm walking down the hall, Callum stops me. "Fredrick. Haud on. Can you give me a moment?"

"Certainly." A flash of guilt has my hand involuntarily swiping my face, hoping to remove any faint traces of his decadent sister from my mouth.

"Great," he says. "Let's talk in the hall." I follow him through the doors.

The Burnes' Norse Garden Estates staff are second to none. The party has only just ended and this room has been cleared, the decorations have been removed, and the hardwoods are gleaming. We sit across from one another at the massive oak trestle table and discuss our nemesis.

The Hoax is a gang which, up until recently, had kept their diabolical people-trafficking ring to the city of Glasgow. With the help of the only disloyal islander in Callum's home, they tried to establish themselves on the shores of the family's island.

Callum and his co-captain, Bayne of the Kings Mafia, who has kept the island safe and isolated from outside crime for nearly a decade, decided it would be best if the Kings created another branch of their crime organization in Glasgow to monitor and, hopefully, one day defeat the Hoax.

Thus, Callum Burnes began the Glasgow arm of the Kings Mafia. Cailean Bayne, known simply as Bayne, rules the island.

Callum recruited young adults from the island who wanted to explore the city to work as eyes and ears for the Kings. As a partner, I've been pulled in, offering my distillery bar and club as hosting grounds to employ the islanders as plants.

I tapped my eager apprentice—a bit of distillery humor for you—and whisky connoisseur Alex to run the distillery.

Sabrina Lopez, a sharp-minded young lady who grew up with five older brothers and thus takes shit from no one, has taken my place running the day-to-day management of Frisky Whisky.

Declan, Callum's right-hand man and a soldier of the Kings, will head the ear-to-the-ground surveillance we run from the West End club, Level Z, where all the players of Glasgow come out to party.

As time has passed, we've recruited trusted locals to join us, and we're united in our efforts to stop the Hoax.

People from all walks of life in Glasgow enjoy my business and delicious whisky.

The warm liquor loosens their tongues and spills their secrets to our pretty plants, who spy for us and report any essential information and minute detail they think might be important or valuable.

Callum and I meet weekly, if not daily, so I can fill him in on my team's findings.

Our conversation lulls. The crackling fire in the Great Hall fills the brief silence. The flickering flames dance shadows on the white walls.

After a moment, Callum brings up the topic at the forefront of his mind.

Freya.

"I'd do anything to keep her safe." His green eyes search my face for understanding.

Being a single child born to a man who thought children were just small-sized adults, I can't fully understand his sibling loyalty. The Kings are the closest thing I have to family. Knowing Freya, though, I fully understand his devotion to her.

"Callum, you worry too much about Freya," I say as I lean back in my chair, the dimly lit room casting shadows across the long table between us. I think of her demanding her panties back from me. "She can hold her own."

Trust me.

"I can't help it, Fredrick," Callum replies. "She's stubborn and reckless, always putting herself in danger without a second thought. I must find someone to protect her and make her see reason."

Callum's piercing green eyes bear into mine, his expression tense with concern for his beloved sister. "I tell her to take the car, and she walks. I tell her to keep her phone on at all times so we can trace her, and she purposefully leaves it in her office when she goes to lunch. I've got eyes and ears on her as much as possible, but it's not enough. Not with the Hoax's numbers growing."

I nod slowly, knowing Freya's independent nature and stubborn refusal to heed warnings all too well. "Aye, brother," I reply, my voice grave with concern. "Freya is a force to be reckoned with, but even the sharpest sword needs a shield."

"I'm the one who'll need a shield when she finds out what I'm planning."

I want to laugh, but his face is lined with despair, so I don't. "Everything is in place. As we discussed, I've found the perfect piece of real estate in Inverness. Bought it months ago. I'm just having Sabrina do her final run-through on the staff we'll be transferring to work for us there."

"You're a true friend, Fredrick. When I came to you asking for help, I thought ye'd think I was a wee bit mad. I'm lucky to have you come to my aid."

We momentarily contemplate the crackling flames, listening to the wood shifting as it burns. "I'll do what I can to help you, Callum," I finally say, reaching across the table to grasp Callum's hand in solidarity. "We'll find someone who can match her fire. Who is strong enough to stand up to her. Someone who can protect her."

Callum gives me a grateful smile, squeezing my hand in return. "Thank you, Fredrick. Your support means the world to me. Tell me about this prime piece of real estate you've purchased for us."

"The estate was first built in the 1800s—" I'll have to fill him in on the details of the property later because, at this moment, the heavy wooden doors of the Great Hall swing open and Freya strides in, her ice-blonde hair cascading down her back like a waterfall. She wears a black silk robe over her slender body and puffy pink slippers on her feet.

There's a rosy flush riding high on her cheekbones, and a cat that's gotten the cream smile rests on her beautiful face—a look put there by my expert tongue. The secret knowledge turns me on.

Her green eyes flash in surprise to find me here with her brother, and the relaxed look is quickly replaced with distrust. "What are you two plotting?" Freya asks, avoiding my gaze.

I hold back from tasting my lips as I watch her.

Callum clears his throat, exchanging a glance with me before speaking. "We were just talking business."

Freya arches an eyebrow at her brother, clearly skeptical as she ignores me. "Is that so?" She crosses her arms over her chest, her expression daring him to continue. "Callum, this little fireside chat better not have anything to do with our conversation before the party."

"Just work talk, Freya." Callum, clearly ready to be out from under her investigative gaze after our conversation, stands, stretching with a yawn. "Fredrick, I'll go find Declan. He can drive you home."

"I'll call my driver." I stand to follow him from the room, bidding her, "Goodnight, Freya. Sweet dreams."

Her arms stay crossed over her chest, one hip and her slim chin jutting out at me with defiance as she finally acknowledges my existence.

"Stay," she demands. "I want to talk to you."

Callum leaves us.

"Alright." I remain standing, casually slipping my hands in my pockets. "What's up?"

She pulls one arm from her chest to point to heaven. "What happened upstairs?"

"Yes?" A sly grin pulls at my mouth as I drag my tongue over my lips for a final taste of her.

"That..." Her arms go back to crossed, a shield to keep me out, but she can't stop the blush that reddens from watching my lips. "Will never. EVER. Happen again."

Having had her say, she turns on her pink-slippered heel like she's wearing five-inch stilettos and strides from the room.

I can't resist her. I can't ignore the heated tension that tugs and pulls between us, no matter how hard I try. Freya is a temptation I can no longer deny, a forbidden fruit I must taste again, even as I assist her brother in finding her a husband.

I need more Freya.

Chapter Five

F reya

I wake with a headache like I've knocked my head against a concrete floor. There was so much ass-shaking at Level Z it's possible I slipped and forgot. Not quite ready for the morning sun slicing through the space between my pale blue damask curtains, I pat my hand around the nightstand, searching for my phone.

I feel something out of place. Whining as I open my eyes to investigate, I glance over at the table. Praise the Lord—just what I need.

"Kathy, housekeeper of the year." Flipping over on my back, I tip back the tablets and electrolyte water she's left on my nightstand. "Make that of the century. Such a dear."

Flopping back down against my massive cloud of feather pillows, I throw an arm over my eyes, attempting to block out the punishing sun. "Och, what a night!"

A fuzzy memory from last night's party at Level Z comes to my aching mind. A strange man with ice blue eyes and a black vine tattoo creeping up his neck, trying to get my attention.

At first, I thought he was hitting on me, but then I had that vague flashback moment where you realize you've seen a person before. He seemed familiar, but I also acknowledged I was wearing Scotch goggles. Even through my alcohol-induced haze, the seriousness in his icy gaze grabbed me.

What did he say? Was he warning me about something? A bartender—one of our Glasgow Kings, a younger man I didn't recognize as an islander—came around the bar and ushered him away before he could get his message to me. Or hit on me. Not sure which.

Prickles crawl across the back of my neck as I kick myself for not paying more attention to him then.

"Pfft. No regrets," I assure myself, moving on.

A smile plays on my lips as I think of the parts I do remember clearly: the dancing and the karaoke contest, the stage lit with florescent pinks and purples, the music thumping loudly. I was singing at the top of my lungs; June and Madyson played backup dancers on stage behind me.

My head pulses, my dehydrated brain squeezing away from my skull, making my stomach nauseous.

Was it worth it? I ask myself. "Hell, yes, it was."

I'd love to spend the day hurkle-durkling, but I've yet to miss a single day of work, and today will not be my first. Between my All Hallows Eve party last Thursday then celebrating last night, I swear to myself I'll not be going out again on a work night for at least—

Who am I kidding?

Finally tracking down my phone, I look at the time. I've got an hour to shower and blow-dry meters of hair, which will also need a deep conditioning treatment since my hairdresser just stripped my medium blonde roots to platinum.

Slap on enough makeup and pull on a suit to look like the powerhouse solicitor I am. Not the hungover slag I currently appear to be.

And after all this—I've got to find a way down that gorgeous curving staircase—my sleek banister polished daily—and long hallway and out that front door without running smack dab into my beast of a brother.

No doubt he'll have something to say that I don't want to hear. Either about my night out, the fact that I'm still unattached, or something equally annoying.

Fifty-five minutes later, hair shining like a mermaid of the sea, I quietly tiptoe my way down the hall, attempting to avoid him.

A deep, familiar voice booms out, "Freya, you smell like a pub," just about startling the wee out of me.

"Smell?" I flip around to face my giant, overprotective brother. "I just washed!"

He crosses his arms over his massive chest—like he needs to make his biceps look any more prominent—and eyes me with that stern brow furrowing his handsome face. I'm a little surprised he's not stroking his beard in contemplation as he takes in my peely-wally complexion.

Cream blusher is an incredible invention, but there's only so much cosmetics can do.

He asks, "How many whiskys did you have last night?"

"Enough to think I sounded good when I hit the high notes of Tina Charles," I say.

He moans. "Not disco."

"I love to love, but my baby loves to dance!" I give him a little taste, swaying my hips, an imaginary mic to my lips. "I'm spinning like a top." I try to do a turn. Still lightheaded from dehydration, I lose my footing.

Callum catches me in his strong arms, righting me. "Never do that move again."

"It was good last night, I swear! Our act was pure dead brilliant!" My exuberance makes my head pound. I put my hand to my forehead. "We came in fourth."

"You were doing karaoke in front of Glasgow and thinking you were brilliant at it? So, you'd had enough whisky to float a boat."

"Or burn down a building." I moan. "My breath hitting one flicker of a flame last night would have taken out the entire club."

"Freya." His green eyes are serious, his voice dropping an octave. "You're partying too much."

For a beat, I let his words sink in. My head is a mess. He may have a wee bit of a point.

Never one to admit when my younger brother is right, I pull the humor card. "Sharp as a tack. You could have been a detective. Then we'd have been a detective and a lawyer instead of a mafia leader and his sidekick, always ready to bail him and his criminal friends out. The parents would be so proud—"

"Freya..." he warns.

"'Course I'm partying! And drinking. I'm young—"

He cuts me off with a very rude, "Almost thirty."

"Och, never tell a girl her age! As I said, I am young, single, and living in the city. Of course, I party! Anyway, last night, I had a great reason to drink too much—not that I need your permission—but we were celebrating."

"What for?" he asks.

"The Maclean case." I plant my hands on my hips, narrowing my gaze. "I told you about it at dinner the night before last, but maybe you were too enamored with your wifey to hear me."

A contented smile stretches over his face. "Home cooking by a fine-looking woman. One of the many benefits of wearing a wedding ring. And thanks to my bride, I'm a much better listener than I used to be. I know exactly which case you're talking about."

"And?" I challenge.

"Wednesday evening, when you were sipping at your stew, and I took the bowl and polished it off for you with a slab of honey wheat bread, you said you had a case before the judge in the morning," he says triumphantly. "Old man Maclean's case."

"No," I correct him. "Jack." I swap out my fading island accent for my fake Los Angeles one. "The young one. The *hawt* one, as Kitt would say."

Callum's face goes blank. See? I knew he wasn't listening. He was elbow-deep in beef stew and had no idea who I was talking about.

"So, it was rescheduled for yesterday morning, and it was Jack, and yes, I won—you should have heard my closing speech, now THAT was pure dead brilliant—and yes, I went out to celebrate with the girls afterward."

He stares at me.

"And if I know the Maclean family, there'll be a lovely fruit basket in the way of a thank you waiting on my desk, and hopefully, there will be some chocolate biscuits hiding under all that healthy stuff—"

Callum's face is going from blank to seriously disturbed, his brow knitting together, his hand touching his beard. "Freya—"

"Callum, I've got to go—"

He grabs my arm, stopping me. "When you said Maclean, I assumed you meant Harold. Not Jack."

"Nope." I shake my head. "It was certainly Jack. I don't think Mr. Maclean could find trouble if it tugged him with a fisherman's hook."

Callum's thick brows knit, his green eyes flashing with worry. "Jack—I thought you said you'd never go against your principles with who you represent."

"I did! And I didn't!" Och, will this man stop talking in circles and let me get to work? "Callum, what are you talking about?"

His voice rumbles like thunder. "He's not who you think he is."

"What do you mean..." The look on his face leaves me with an uneasy feeling wiggling into my already queasy stomach. "Tell me."

"The elder, he's fine, he's a good man. But your Jack." His eyes go cold. "The young one...whatever he was accused of, I assure you, he's guilty."

"No," I say, my heart dropping into the soles of my stilettos. "Can't be."

"Why not?" He eyes me. "'Cause he's good-looking?"

I shake my head, denying that the man's classic Highland smoldering good looks have anything to do with my assessment of his story and the facts he presented to my team during interviews.

Sure, it was very last-minute—his lawyer dropped out of the case moments before he was due in court—but I trusted my gut, rescheduled him for yesterday, and got him off.

"I'm a terrific judge of people," I say, wondering if I did, in fact, let the man's strong jawline and thick hair sway me. Having pin-straight hair that won't curl myself, I admire a wavy head of hair. "And the Macleans are as clean as the word in their surname."

"Things have changed. We need to talk." He gives me that look that means I will do what he says, especially since he's not yet let go of my arm. He's distraught. "No more putting me off. Tonight."

The man with the blue eyes comes to mind. Should I mention him to Callum? A little yellow parakeet pops out of the grandfather clock in the hall I'd had shipped in from Norway, tweeting his sweet little tune, informing me I'm going to be late.

I push the memory away with a sigh. "Fine. Tonight. But I really must go."

Something heavy in his tone makes me take a beat, assess his tight jaw and the death grip he's still got on my bicep. "Promise me you'll come straight home from work. And take our car service. Don't walk."

"Car service? You mean your band of thugs?" Finally, I head toward the door, my back to him. I offer an eye roll and a joke to lighten the mood. "My little brother. So paranoid."

But the air stays heavy as I leave, and I feel his gaze on me as I go.

I let his guards drive me to work, but as much as he'd like to, Callum knows full well that he can't control me. Nor I, him. I let the tension of the morning go as I breeze through the office, greeting the others.

Everyone was at the club last night, singing karaoke or trying out their VR or indoor glow-in-the-dark mini-golf, but all drinking too much. We have sore heads and our tails tucked between our legs, so the morning is quiet.

At noon, I order lunch from the deli on the corner to be delivered to my desk: two Diet Cokes and a tuna on rye. I pick at the sandwich but eat the crisps.

Women think I'm thin because I don't eat, but it's not true. My friends know I eat plenty. Only just what I want. Do you know how many calories are in a full dinner? Please, I'd rather have dessert.

I didn't eat Fiona's beef stew at dinner the other night, but I downed about half a loaf of the warm bread she had baked, slathered in the butter she had brought in from Bayne cows.

I pop two more headache tablets and wash them back with the soda. The hazy memory of the man at the bar warning me last night comes back to me. As does my run-in with Callum this morning.

I'm dreading our talk tonight.

Callum's words from this morning have me questioning my choices but everyone at the firm seems as enamored with Jack as I was.

I mean, not enamored per say. That's not why I took his case. My minge doesn't rule my brain.

Further evidence to prove my point I let him who we do not speak of do what we do not speak of to me. I dove into the pleasure, reveled in it, then told him that was all there would be between us. And forgot all about him.

Mostly.

Pressing my thighs together, I ignore the heat between my legs just like I push away the memory of Fredrick's tongue between my thighs...what feels like every five minutes for the past week.

Five o'clock on the dot, June breezes by my desk. She wears a red trench coat belted around her waist, a sleek black Chanel bag over her shoulder, clearly leaving for the day. "Girl, you were on fire last night! The host didn't want to take the microphone back. You brought the house down."

"We did!" I laugh. "Couldn't have done it without my backup dancers."

"Speaking of last night, what did that guy want?" she asks.

"What guy?"

"The one with the weird blue eyes." Her nose scrunches. "They were, like, abnormally light."

"Oh, him." The prickles return to the back of my neck. "Dunno."

Already bored with the man, she shrugs, changing the subject. "Madyson and I still have insane headaches from last night, and there's only one cure for an afternoon hangover."

"Hair of the dog!" we say in unison.

Madyson shows up, perching the curve of her cute ass on the edge of my desk. "What's a Hera the dog?" she asks.

"The *hair* of the dog, which is short for 'the hair of the dog that bit you,'" I inform. "And the nickname of the first drink you have the next day to cure your hangover."

Madyson says, "So you'll join us? June and I are headed to the pub for a drink."

I can taste the sweet relief of an ice-cold bright-pink Manhattan on the tip of my tongue. Callum's stern green eyes butt into my daydream, reminding me of my promise to him.

I close down my computer for the day. "I can't. I've got this family thing."

June's eyes light up. "Invite Fiona! Everyone loves your sister-in-law."

"Please do," Madyson adds. "I swear, I haven't seen her in ages."

I roll my eyes, confessing, "My brother keeps that girl on lockdown. Fiona can hold her own, but she seems perfectly happy being stuck at the house feeding him. No—it's something with Callum anyway."

June's eyes twinkle with mischief. "That Viking of a man could lock me up to anything, anytime."

"Och! Gross, June!" I shake my head at her. "That's my flesh and blood."

"And some damn fine-looking flesh, too. Those eyes, that hair, those legs—"

"His or mine?" I laugh.

"Both! I swear the two of you could be models. Fiona is SOOOOO lucky. I swear I'd hate her if she weren't so damn sweet." Madyson slides off my desk, layering on the peer pressure as she eyes me. "Are you coming out?"

"I can't—"

"One drink." Madyson sticks out her pouty lower lip.

June pleads, "One drink. Pleeeeeeeeeease?"

Madyson adds, "Pretty, pretty please?"

"How is it that all you Americans are so damn persuasive?"

"Why do you think we work in law?" June grabs the gold chain of my Stella McCartney Falabella tote, lifting it from the desk. "You're coming with us to O'Malley's. Let's go. Right now. Come on!"

Callum's overprotective. I know he's worried. But here with my friends, our conversation this morning seems a million lifetimes ago.

And as the Americans at my office say, if I give him an inch, he'll take a mile.

Plus, Madyson is halfway out the door with my brand-new

bag in her greedy hands. If I don't save it, she'll switch our bags out at the pub and wear my Stella to work tomorrow.

"Fine!" I call out, beaten. I race after them. "ONE drink!"

A quarter of an hour later, I sit with the girls, laughing, fruity pink drinks between us.

My phone rings. Callum. I greet him after answering, but he offers no hello and says, "Why aren't you home?"

"Just nipped down to the pub for a quick drink with the girls," I say. "But I will take the car service home. Promise."

"Where are you?" he demands.

"Why?" I hesitate, but eventually, the uneasy silence demands I tell him. I sigh out, "O'Malley's."

He snaps, "I'll be right there."

"What?" I almost lunge from my seat as if I can stop him from here. "Don't!"

Of course, he's already hung up. I don't want a scene. Things between the Burnes siblings can get heated. I need to get out of here.

Now.

Rising from my stool, I throw a twenty on the table. "Look, girls, I'm sorry, but I've got to go."

"Uh-oh. Twelve o'clock." Madyson nods to the door behind my back.

I turn around to find my brother's large frame filling the entryway of O'Malley's. He's already here. How is that possible?

"See you tomorrow!" Grabbing my bag, I rush to greet him before he can join us at the table.

I hear Madyson's whispered sigh behind me as I go. "Fiona's such a lucky girl..."

I run straight out the door onto the street, nearly bumping into Callum. "What are you doing here? And how did you get here so fast?"

"I came to your office to pick you up myself, but you'd already left." What he says next makes my blood run ice cold. "He's not just guilty, Freya." My brother's matching green eyes slice into mine. "Jack Maclean is a member of the Hoax."

"The Hoax?"

Just repeating the name of the dangerous, filthy, people-trafficking ring that runs out of my beautiful, beloved city of Glasgow makes my stomach sink right to the soles of my black peep-toe ankle-strap slingbacks.

"Aye. One and the same." The disappointment in his gaze causes me physical pain. Sure, I worry him from time to time. Piss him off daily. But I've never let him down like this.

"And I represented him." My voice comes out strange, sounding far away.

Callum nods, confirming the fear he can read creeping into my face. "And now everyone thinks you're one of *them.*"

"No..." My words are swallowed by a desperate moan echoing in my ears. It's coming from me. Desperate, I grab each of his arms in my hands. "I had NO idea Jack was with them. Please! Tell me you believe me."

He stares at me with pain. "Freya..."

No. Not Callum. It KILLS me that anyone from the island would think this of me, but my own flesh and blood? My baby brother? It's too much.

"You believe me, right?" I grip him tighter, trying to shake him, but he's a marble statue. "Tell me you believe me."

He stares down at the ground between us. My pulse is racing; he waits a beat too long. Finally, he says, "Aye. I believe you." A rush of relief fills me. It's gone as quickly as it came with what he says next. He drags his sad gaze back up to meet mine. "But how could ye not know, Freya?"

Standing in front of O'Malley's, my brother's question hanging between us, a part of me dies.

Chapter Six

F redrick

CALLUM DID HIS BEST TO KEEP TABS ON FREYA, BUT his dedicated team would be stretched thin if they investigated every case she took. The Maclean clan made their request at the last minute, only after their lawyer pulled out.

Freya's got Jack Maclean off. He's a recently initiated member of the Hoax. Too recent for Freya to know about unless she investigated him thoroughly.

Rumors have begun swirling all over Scotland that the sibling power duo of Callum and Freya Burnes has split their allegiances. Falsehoods that Callum is still co-running the Kings with Cailean Baynes. Lies that Freya is now casting her lot with the lowlife of Glasgow, the Hoax.

The misinformation couldn't be further from the truth.

Callum and Freya are as strong as ever, loyal only to the Kings. However, when Freya finds out about Callum's hand in her future, there will be strain between the green-eyed siblings. But Callum says he'd "take her rage over her harm any day."

He says the Burnes are quick to anger but forgive quickly.

Let's hope that's true for the sake of their relationship. I'm in the Great Hall at Norse Garden to finalize the details of our agreement. The Viking of a man is waiting for me, a tray with a French press between us. The aroma of rich coffee made the correct way gives me a pang for home. I take a seat.

Callum fills my cup. "Thanks for coming as quickly as you could."

We start with the smaller topics, and I tell him what my employees have heard.

I share the most essential information to begin with. "Tavish Wilson, the bartender at Level Z, remember him?"

He casts his mind back briefly before saying, "The good-looking one that all the bartenders work harder for. The one the younger female servers get distracted by?"

"That's the one. We've had to monitor the waitresses' times to pick up drinks for the customers in the VIP room and make them place their orders with all the bartenders equally, not just with Tavish."

Callum lists off what he knows of Tavish. "Newer recruit, eager, loyal, moving up quickly." His tone drops. "Lost a younger sister to the Hoax's people-trafficking ring."

"Hence his enthusiasm for our work. He's an outstanding

young man. And he is proving to be quick on his feet. He had some interesting news for me," I say. "About Freya."

"Pray tell." He sighs, leaning his large frame back in his tall wooden chair. "Or don't." He drums his fingertips against the tabletop. "I'm worried sick about that girl. I don't know how much more I can take."

I press on, knowing he needs this information. "Tavish was working the bar Thursday night at Level Z. Around nine o'clock, Freya and a group of her female co-workers came into the club"—turning heads and drawing attention as beautiful, well-dressed women tend to do—"just after one of Jack Maclean's mates. He goes by Ross Macdonald—"

His thick brow furrows. "The one with the light blue eyes?"

"Yes." I nod. "The same."

He asks, "We've had surveillance on him for a while now, aye?"

I confirm. "Six months. Ever since we got word that he'd joined the Hoax."

"Tavish saw Ross come in fifteen minutes before the girls. He served him a whisky and watched him plant himself at the end of the bar. Tavish said Ross's eyes were constantly on the door as if he were waiting for someone. When the girls came in, Ross stood, grabbed his drink, and moved to the center of the bar."

"To wait there for the girls, knowing they'd order drinks first," Callum says.

"They always do." The solicitors always order drinks within five minutes of entering my establishments. And my God, how they can hold their liquor. It's impressive. "Ross was trying to get Freya's attention at the bar. Freya paid him a moment of mind while Tavish decided how long he'd let it go on for."

He does the classic Callum move—his hand smoothing over his beard to calm himself. "'Course Freya was friendly-like with him. She's never met a stranger; every man in the bar saw her talk to him. They had eyes on those women from the moment they walked in."

"Right." I share the conclusion I'd come to. "In the eyes of Glasgow, Freya got Jack Maclean off, went straight home to get all dolled up, then met the girls to celebrate the win—"

He groans. "Freya out on the town, celebrating a win for the Hoax."

"A win for the Hoax," I agree.

Pain and frustration crack his typically stoic demeanor as he heaves a sigh.

Knowing he'll need every upsetting detail, I continue. "Then we have Ross MacDonald coming in a bit before her as if he was waiting for her."

"And Freya being Freya," he fills in, "spoke to him for at least a few moments, I'm sure. The place was packed. Everyone saw the two of them together."

"And that's when Tavish decided that any information that could be gathered from their conversation wasn't worth leaving Freya talking openly with a member of the Hoax for another moment. And escorted Ross from the bar," I finish.

"I'm thankful for that," he says. "Let's bring Tavish closer into the circle."

I nod. "I agree. And I've passed along your gratitude to him."

"Thank you." He runs his hand through his hair, leaving it mussed. Slamming a closed fist on the table, he says, "Damn, how I wish we could keep that trash out of our places altogether, but then we'd never get the information we need."

But we both know the issue at hand tonight isn't the Hoax. It's Freya.

I sit quietly, sipping coffee, giving him time to process. Finally, he says, "She's gone too far this time, Fredrick."

My heart rate picks up, and my blood heats. What he will ask of me, I'm ready and willing for. "I'm here to help you in any way I can."

His eyes meet mine. "You know what I need."

I do. And I need the same.

"Callum." I sit back in my chair. "You have to be sure. There is no going back with me. Ever."

"That's why I've chosen you. You know what forever means." His gaze stays steady. "Have you prepared everything like I asked of you?"

I nod. "I have."

"And you're willing?"

"Of course I am."

Relief comes over him, the tension in his broad shoulders easing. "Thank you, Fredrick. You truly have become a brother to me. I trust you with more than my own life."

I swallow back the lump in my throat. Loyalty to the Kings fulfilled me. Now, I have a deep need to protect Freya as well. "I consider it an honor."

He has no idea how long I've been willing to enact his plan.

From the moment I saw her, I wanted her. Until now unable to give her anything other than cunnilingus, this is the only way I can have her without having to involve that sickly, terrifying thing I hate most in this world.

Love.

Luckily, Callum's asked me nothing of that nonsense. He wants a protector, a defender who would put his sister's life before their own. And as he said, he needs someone who knows the meaning of forever, which is one value I've taken from my staunch Catholic upbringing.

We rise to bid our farewells—what? Those heavy doors fly open just like All Hallows Eve after the party.

Freya comes striding in.

Callum and I stand there, bucks in headlights.

Her gaze goes from him to me. "Oh! You two cohorts again."

Tension tightens in the air between the three of us. How much has she heard? I assure myself the doors are thick and solid. We kept our voices low.

Freya's taste has become part of me, a fragrant melody that calls to me like a siren's song. It's been far too long since I've touched her. Standing in the same room with her and not being able to taste her is torture.

"I'll leave you two to talk," I say, unsure of how much Callum is willing to tell her. It's not my place to inform her of our plan.

"No, stay. Let's us three talk." He walks around the table, joining Freya and me.

Freya stands with her arms at her sides, elegantly dressed in a sleeveless black shift, her hair contrasting as it falls down her back. Refusing to look my way. She wants me gone. "What would the three of us possibly have to discuss tonight?"

"There's no easy way to say this," Callum starts. "Freya, ye have to get away from Glasgow. It's the safest thing for ye, ken?"

"No." She shakes her head, aghast. Her long, loose hair swishes over her back. "I'm not leaving our Norse Garden. That would further the gossip, make people think I must be with the Hoax, that there is some fracture between the Burnes siblings, which couldn't be further from the truth—"

"Excuse me, my Lady," I say. "I could cut the tension between the two of you with a butter knife."

"Well, yes," she concedes without acknowledging me, "we're in a wee bit of a disagreement right now, sure," she flips her long hair over her shoulder, "but nothing like me joining ANOTHER gang. The men of the Kings are just as much my brothers as they are yours, Callum. Don't ye forget it."

Callum stresses his point. "I know, Freya, and they look upon you like a sister just the same. Which is why Bayne and I agree—"

She cuts him off, shouting, lava in her tone. "Haud yer wheesht, brother."

"Freya," I warn, pulling her back.

She still doesn't look at me but lowers her voice. "I can't believe you talked to Bayne about this. We can handle this on our own. You've no need to get the island involved."

Callum raises his. "'Course I have. It's your life we're talking about, Freya."

"My...life?"

"Aye, your life," he says more quietly.

"What do you mean, my life, Callum? Don't tell me any of the islanders believe a word of this Hoax nonsense. That would kill me quicker than any thug."

He strokes his beard. "No. God no. I hope..."

"You hope?" Her voice squeaks in disbelief.

"They've seen you at the court with Jack," I say, helping Callum. "They've seen the man you talked to at the club.

"A man did talk to me at the club and tried to tell me something, but your men ushered him away." She's adamant. "He approached me. Not the other way around." Her green eyes slowly turn to meet mine. "I'd like a word alone with my brother. Do you mind?"

"Actually," I address Freya. "I'd like a word with you first."

Callum gives me a knowing look; we've already had our discussion. He turns to leave the room, Freya calling after him. "Callum, wait! I have more I want to say to you."

"Later, Freya. Walk with me, Fredrick." Callum says.

I walk with him to the door of the Great Hall. As we part, he offers me a firm handshake. Our eyes lock. What we've agreed to is now set in stone and the handshake we've shared has set things in motion. He's ready for me to tip the first domino.

The transfer of power has begun.

The door closes behind Callum. We're alone. The room is silent. We stand only an arm's length apart, but I won't reach for her. She must close the space between us herself.

"Freya," I say, every bit of heat from me pouring out of my gaze. "Come here."

She crosses her arms over her chest with a haughty, "I am here."

"Come," I say. "To me."

Warily, she eyes me. Finally, she offers, "Being alone in a room with you is dangerous enough. I'll stay where I stand."

Never breaking our gaze, I wait.

An internal battle rages inside her, one she's quickly losing. Something shifts in her eyes, a flush rising on her face. And without a word, she slides over to me, closing the space between us.

I want to call her my good girl, to take her into my arms, smooth her silky hair down her back, and whisper sweet words to her.

I have so much to learn about her, her preferences, which touches will make her melt like butter in my hand. Instead, I think of something I've done once before and not been slapped, a touch she softened to.

I cup her face in my hand, her skin cool against mine. I stroke my thumb over her bottom lip. At my touch, her lashes flutter a touch, betraying her before she steels her gaze, saying, "Don't touch me."

She doesn't pull away.

I want to laugh. I don't. I drag my thumb down, her lip popping up, then resting it on the cup of her chin. I know she's scared; recent events turned her life upside down. She's not bitten me yet, so I take my chances, moving slowly as I did with a feral kitten I once saved from a storm drain. I slip my other hand along her face, sliding fingers through her silky hair and holding her.

I lean in, reassuring her. "Everything will be alright, Freya. They'll come to their senses. They know your loyalty."

Finally, she relents, breaks, and allows me to bring her closer as she rests her face on my chest, releasing a shaky sigh as she won't allow herself to cry. Wrapping my arms around her, I hold her. "I can ease your mind," I say. "I can make you feel better."

"Nothing but clearing my name will make this better."

I bring my mouth to her ear, whispering, "But I can make you feel better *now*. For a few moments at least." Softly, I kiss her cheek. "Let me."

She gives a soft moan. "No."

"Yes." The hand I have on her back trails down lower, resting on the scoop of her waist, pressing her lithe body hard against me. I know she feels my hardness, my desire for her pulsing against her.

"No."

Strands of her hair stick to my mouth as I murmur, "Yes." I nuzzle against the curve at the base of her neck. I run my fingers over her shoulder, pushing her hair back and exposing her pale skin. I brush my lips over the nape of her neck.

"No," she moans; the soft sound of her pleasure makes me grow harder, and I pull her tighter into me. Her head arches back, giving me access to the sensitive area of her delicate skin.

I kiss her, sucking, nipping, leaving the first of my marks on her flawless skin. "Yes." Many more will come as I explore every inch of her. I am a patient man; soon, she'll be all mine. I'll have a lifetime to discover her, and I'll never tire of her taste.

I smooth down her side, over her stomach, brushing over her breast—

She snatches up my hand, tearing it away from her breast. "No."

I pause. This time, the no is different. The air in the room shifts. She won't meet my eye, her flush growing more profound as she shifts her weight. Something with that touch wasn't right. I need her to know she can trust me. With her mind, her body, her life.

I bring her hand to my lips, softly kissing her fingers. "I understand," I say.

Needing to get her back to that relaxed, loose, sultry place of pleasure, I take her other hand in mine, so now I'm holding both of hers.

I guide her carefully, her taking backward steps until we've reached the nearest wall, resting her back against it. Firelight dances over her stunning face as she watches me, intrigued by me.

I lift her arms, holding them stretched out as I stare down at her, burying my eyes into hers. "You never have to explain yourself to me. But if I do anything, anything at all, that doesn't feel good, feel right, you tell me. *Tu comprends*? You understand?"

She gives a quick nod, looking away.

I press her wrists against the wall, pinning them in place above her head. I kiss her forehead, her right cheek, her left cheek. Her breath hitches, and her mouth tilts as if searching for mine, wanting to be kissed.

Not yet.

I'm saving our first kiss. For a time when she's proven she fully trusts me.

Instead, I tease her with kisses down her neck, over her collarbone. I switch to one hand, circling her wrists, keeping her arms imprisoned against the wall. My now free hand trails down her belly. She quivers under my touch. I watch her face illuminated by light as her head lolls back, her chin tilting up to heaven as her eyes flutter closed. She's exposed the smooth curve of her pale neck, and I move in, tasting the skin with the tip of my tongue.

I find the hem of her dress and sneak underneath, feeling the silky material of the black tights she wears underneath. I moan, my erection uncomfortable and tight against my trousers. I press it against one of her thighs as my fingers glide up the other, stroking the satin panties that hide under the tights.

I rub her gently at first, slowly, listening to her breathing and her moans, adjusting my touch and my pace to pleasure her. She shifts her weight, pressing her back against the wall. I want to kiss her, to taste her, but I can't tear my gaze away from her face, watching the pleasure ease her worry, the way her beautiful pale arms stretch out above her as she moves.

So beautiful. So strong. I want her, need her. And I will have her.

I need another taste.

I struggle with the elastic of the waist of her tights, finally getting my fingers to her bare skin. "I want to feel how wet you are for me, princess."

"Yes." She pushes her hips forward, begging for my touch.

I finger her, moaning at her slickness. "Beautiful woman, so wet for me, so ready to come for me like you did in your bedroom with my tongue between your thighs." Her soft skin is velvety beneath my fingers. I fill her with two fingers, stroking her, moving in and out of her, as I thumb her swollen clit.

"Yes. Yes." Her back arches hard, her chin jutting high, her smooth voice quietly crying out, "Fredrick."

"I love the way you say my name. I love the sound you make when you come." I increase my pace, moving against her hips as they roll and buck against me, her body working with my hand to bring her to climax.

She comes hard against my hand, her muscles tightening around my fingers, her head flying forward as she bites back a scream, her teeth sinking into her bottom lip.

I whisper against her ear, speaking to her in French, a language she doesn't speak. What I say translates to, *Soon I'll have you all to myself, and I'll make you scream as loud as you can, and I'll never let you hold back.*

She shudders, folding at the waist as well as she can, imprisoned by my hand as she is. I release her, and her arms fall to her sides as if she's taking a bow at the finale to her climax. I pull my hand from her clothing, bringing my fingers to my mouth. I catch her eye, and she watches me, her gaze filling with shame, her cheeks flushed with desire as I slip my fingers into my mouth.

Sweet Freya honey. Drawing my fingers from my mouth, I lick my lips. "I'm addicted to your taste."

"You're...so..."

"What?"

"I don't know," she breathes. She shakes her head, pressing her hands against my chest to push me away. "But I want you gone. I need to talk to my brother. Leave me. Now. Go."

"When you speak to him, remember, everything he asks of you is only out of his love for you." I cup her face, letting her breathe in her own sweet scent. I lean in, pausing momentarily, my lips a beat away from hers, before placing a chaste kiss on her cheek.

I adjust my trousers and go to leave her.

She calls Callum's name as she crosses the room. Callum passes by me, entering the room as I leave. He and I exchange a glance. I stand at the open doorway as he meets her at the table.

There's silence between them. I pull the door closed behind me. The conversation starts smoothly, their voices low and murmuring through the door. I grin to myself, proud that I was the one who could tame Freya Burnes.

A moment later, they lay into one another. *La veche!* The Burnes do burn as hot as the islanders say.

Taming will take time, like breaking a wild horse, though I'd never want to change her. Only have her soften toward me. With a newfound purpose in my gait, I stride down the hall, the echoes of Callum and Freya arguing behind me.

Soon, I'll have all the time in the world. The handshake between Callum and me solidified that fact. Freya now belongs to me. I'll leave nothing to chance. I'll place the diamond crown on her head, ensuring Freya becomes the powerful Mafia wife I know she was born to be.

I know she won't come willingly. For now, at least, she'll be *ma femme mafieuse captive.*

My captive Mafia wife.

Chapter Seven

THE MORNING OF FREYA'S ARRIVAL
AT WEE INVERNESS...

F reya

CALLUM HAS TO BELIEVE ME THAT I HAD NO IDEA Jack was with the Hoax. Had I known, I never would have taken his case! Now he thinks I'm in danger, which is only going to add fuel to the crazy get-Freya-a-husband notion he's been dwelling on.

The concept is so ludicrous that I move on to one that has my heart sinking into my slippers.

Do my people honestly think I've betrayed them?

Late last night, wearing PJs and face masks, curled up in my many layers of duvets, Fiona assured me over tea and biscuits that everything was fine and Callum was just being overprotective when he said I need to leave Norse Garden—

"Though why not consider it, Freya? Two back-to-back intense trials—couldn't you use a vacation after all?"

And on the topic of our beloved islanders—

"Of course they're confused, they have questions, but sure, they're behind you...'

I found the chocolate the biscuit was dipped in more comforting than her words, told her I was tired, would be fine on my own, and sent her to bed. Fiona and I usually have no secrets, but I didn't even tell her about what had happened with Fredrick just hours before in the Great Hall.

This morning, I've silenced numerous calls from home, unsure of what Carol Ann and the others would ask me, knowing I'd be too brokenhearted to defend myself if they doubted me. And Callum...it's too painful to remember our conversation outside of O'Malley's, so I don't, shoving it down into the darkest part of myself.

An angry tear of hurt comes to my eyes, and I brush it away. They know me. We've grown up together, bandaged each others skinned knees, stolen beer, and smoked together. Hell, in our awkward stages of teenage lust, I kissed half of the Kings, I'm sure of it.

How could they ever doubt me, for a moment—me, Freya Burnes, the head female of our Burnes clan?

And my flesh and blood...

No matter what any fresh meat Glasgow Kings told me about an islander, I'd deny it to the grave, have that brother's back, take it public, and make it right. I don't believe in whispered words behind closed doors. That is what I love about court. All the facts are out in the open, free to be disputed by anyone, but in the end...

Only the facts stand in the end.

Pushing all the yuckiness away, I try to improve my mood, distract myself, and focus on something else. Sweets. I pull on a cozy gray waffle-knit robe over my silk black button-down long-sleeve pajama top and matching flowy pants and tie it around my waist. Under the advice of my mirror, I pop some 24k gold gel stickies over the black circles under my eyes.

"Stress is so NOT my beauty product of choice." I slip my bare feet into my puffy pink slippers and wander out of my room, searching out my breakfast.

The newlyweds are out all day for their once-per-week preplanned Saturday outing. Today, I think they're hiking to a meadow for a picnic. How boring! They seem obsessed with themselves, never having their hands off one another.

Honestly, it's so adorable I could vomit.

Although alone, I CAN have a nice day to myself. I can recover from the confusing sex-plosion in the Great Hall with Fredrick. The hurt I feel from the Kings' mistrust—the guilt over disappointing Callum and the fact that he wants me to leave our precious Norse Garden.

My slippered feet pad over the gleaming marble floors to our oversized commercial fridge, which I sort through, looking for sweets to comfort me. The house staff is off today, but I find a plate left for me: fruit, cheese, bread, and thinly sliced beef.

Behind that is a thick slice of chocolate cake.

I grab the small glass dessert plate and push the real food out of the way. "Yes, please!"

I curl up on the comfy gray sofa in the TV room, cake in my lap, hot tea beside me, a lineup of true crime documentaries ready to fill my day. I click on the television, filling the space with my voice. "If anyone hasn't seen the one on the Sherri Papini case, you must. If possible, go in completely blind for best shock value." I sigh. "I really must stop talking to myself."

As much as I brag about being a strong, independent woman, I loathe spending time alone. If Fiona were here, I'd charm her into playing a game of Scrabble with me, Callum grumbling in the corner.

Champers jangles into the room, her prissy paws barely touching the floor as she approaches me. "Here, baby! Come cuddle me!" Gently, I pat the open cushion beside me so as not to scare her away.

As per usual, the cat, who I've secretly nicknamed Ginger for her cream and orange coat, gives me a prudent sniff, looks around for Fiona, then turns and leaves the room, haughtily sticking her fluffy tail up in the air, giving me a glamorous view of her pink bum.

She hates me.

"Fine. More cake for me, Ging." Can cats even have chocolate? The prongs of my fork slice through the creamy ganache layer in the center of the cake just as there's a knock at the door.

I wait for a guard to answer. Prickles dance down the back of my neck, tickling my spine as I wait. Nothing. Another knock. Callum, totally overprotective at every turn, has left me home alone with no guards.

"This is crazy." Grabbing my phone from my robe pocket, I hastily text him.

. . .

Me: Callum, where are the guards

Someone is at the door.

I tap a black lacquered fingernail against my phone screen while waiting for his reply. My heart beats hard at the sound of the next knock.

Callum: Forgot to tell you the guards have a training today

You told me in our screaming match you can take care of yourself

Can you open a door

"Och! Little brothers...I swear..." I punch the words in.

Me: Don't be that way

Can you at least tell me who is at the door before I get up

Ginger doesn't want me to disrupt her for nothing

C: Who is ginger

Whoops!

. . .

Me: Champers

C: I've pulled up the camera
It's just the delivery man of Fredricks
He's dropping something off

FREDRICK FRISQUE WITH THE FRISKY TONGUE. Och! What I wouldn't give to keep that man off my mind.

I set the cake on the side table, toss my fuzzy blanket to the side, and harumph my way down the long hall to the front door, passing by Her Majesty. She's relocated from the TV room as far from me as possible, now curled up in my red velvet foyer chair.

"Don't worry, Ginger! I'll get the door. You relax."

Fully expecting the kind older man, Ian, our usual delivery person, I fling the front door open without looking through the peephole first. On the stoop stands a shorter man wearing a gray pinstriped suit, gelled-back black hair, and a thick mustache.

There's a small red cube-shaped gift box sitting on his open palm. He holds it out closer to me. "For you, madame."

The married version of ma'am in French.

"It's mademoiselle," I assure him. "With absolutely no plans to be addressed as *madame.*"

Instead of correcting himself, he only offers a funny smile.

What a strange man. I take the box, thank him, and close the door.

Triple locking it.

I pad back to my seat, sticking my tongue out at Ginger as I pass, and open the delicate box.

"Oh my gosh! What is this?"

Inside sits a tiny red-and-orange hot air balloon made of thin, colorful paper pasted over a grid of delicate metal forming the balloon—a perfect replica of the one I hired to float above our home two All Hallows Eves ago, tethered to the ground and rising so you could overlook the sparkling lights of the city with one of my themed cocktails in your hand.

Callum said there were no hot air balloons this year. It's a security issue. He said he can only keep what's inside our stone walls safe, which is precisely why he never wants Fiona to leave Norse Garden.

I hold the delicate object by its tiny straw basket, which looks to have been handwoven, admiring the artist's attention to detail. A darling miniature of Champers sits in the basket, complete with her ginger-colored fur. Her cute little face is a replica, and she's even wearing a pink collar with an itty-bitty silver bell.

"This is unreal." I scour my mind, thinking of the local artists I know, wondering who could have created such a piece.

I can't think of anyone.

To say I'm impressed would be an understatement, but coming from my snake-tongued fast-fingered arch-nemesis, I can't admit what a wonderful creation he's produced.

A note flutters out of the box. An invitation? As I read the paper, I realize the words aren't so much a polite request as a demand.

Join me at my estate in Inverness

Wear wedding attire.

"Ha ha! As if!" Letting the paper slip from my fingers, I sigh, watching it flutter to the floor. I've clarified to all parties involved that I will NOT be leaving Norse Garden Estates. "So funny I forgot to laugh, Freddie."

The hot air balloon, on the other hand, I nestle lovingly back into its box. No matter the sender, the little work of art is a treasure.

I'm just getting into the part when Sherri, wrapped in chains, flags down a truck driver on the side of the road to save her from her captors when there's a SECOND knock on our front door.

Holding in a groan, I text Callum AGAIN.

ME: ANOTHER KNOCK

who is THAT

C: FREDRICKS MAN AGAIN

ME: THE WEIRD LITTLE MUSTACHED MAN

what does he want NOW

. . .

C: HE NEEDS TO PICK SOMETHING UP

answer the door

ME: YOU DIDN'T SAY PLEASE

C: ANSWER THE DOOR FREYA

"Geeze, oh man, Callum. Keep your pants on."

Despite my better judgment, I pad my way back over to the door. Stachio is waiting on the stoop. Leaning against the doorframe, I ask breezily, "Can I help you? Callum said you're here to collect something?"

A look of confusion is on his face. "I'm here to collect you," he announces matter-of-factly.

"Collect me?" I gape at his audacity. "Like a suitcase or a bag of old clothes to be donated? What on Earth do you mean by 'collect me?'"

"You've been invited to the Frisque estate in Inverness."

"The note in the box? I thought that was a JOKE."

His caterpillar brow folds. "So, you *have* received Mr. Frisque's invitation."

Pfft! "If you call that an invitation," I say.

"You've had plenty of time to get ready." He eyes my messy bun, the gold gel patches I've placed under my eyes to calm the last of the dark circles, the cozy robe I wear, and most likely a chocolate frosting smudge somewhere on my person. His gaze lowers, taking in the pink tops of my fuzzy slippers. "Are you?"

"Am I what?" I ask, still in shock over his arrival.

He says, "Ready to go?"

"Certainly not! And I'll advise you to leave my property at once." I go to close the door. To my shock, his strong arm shoots out, grabbing the edge of the door to stop me from closing it.

Then, he steps inside. The mustache had me off guard, but now I see this man's full size and strength. He's barely my height but muscled like childhood drawings of the strongman from Fossett's Circus.

My heart hammers in my eardrums as the heat of panic rises in my chest. "What—what are you doing?"

My pulse takes flight, beating like a hummingbird's wings as I back from the door. The guards are at a meeting. The staff have left for the day. The newlyweds aren't even close to coming home yet and are probably pulled over shagging in the back of their Escalade SUV.

And Ginger does nothing. She's still sitting on the velvet chair, daintily licking an already perfectly groomed paw.

I am absolutely, utterly alone. The next house is acres away. We made sure we had complete privacy when we bought the place. There's no point in even screaming. No one will hear me.

"Look. Whatever you want, I'll give it to you, just step outside. Please. I have cash." Whipping over my shoulder, I grab the coffee cash from my shiny black hot-girl fanny pack, shoving it at him. "Here. Take this and go outside. I'll get you more."

"The Frisque family is *generational* wealth," he says, as if I do not know such a thing. "They pay me well." He shakes his head, that seedy grin coming back to his face. "I'm not here for your money."

"What are you here for, then?" I ask.

"You." This time when he speaks, his tone is stern. My blood chills at his following words. "I'm not leaving this house without you."

"Wait here."

"With pleasure." His mustache lifts with his icy smile.

Even his henchman is infuriating. Storming back to the TV room, I grab my phone and scroll through my contacts. Ol' Freddie's at the bottom of my call list—the only time I've rung him was to set up the meeting last month to choose the whisky for the party.

His name is saved as *Fredrick Frisque BEST Distiller in Scotland*.

His attention to detail and need for perfection make him the best in the business. However, this will need to change. In my anger, my thumbs fly over my screen. "Fixed it."

Triumphant, I press the new contact, *Freaky Freddie*—really, everyone should aspire to my level of petty—and wait for him to answer before storming back to the foyer with Ginger and Strongman.

He picks up on the first ring like he's expecting my call. His smooth voice sluices through the line. "Bonjour, madame."

"It's MAD-mo-zell and why is your Frisky Whisky thug standing in the foyer of my house? Are you accosting me in my jammies? Disturbing the cat, who, might I add, is already very jumpy from being home alone this morning?" I pet the cat's soft fur, cooing, "It's okay, Gingy. I'm getting rid of the bad man…"

She swipes a paw at me.

Fredrick clears his throat. "I take it you received my invitation."

"I received a scrap of paper. No name, no timeframe, and no polite request for my presence. Though," I add despite myself, "the artistry of the balloon, I must admit, was second to none."

"I'm glad you like the gift," he says. "And I apologize if you found my manners lacking."

"Lacking? Pfft! Non-existent, I'm afraid, Mr. Frisque."

"A lovely gift accompanied with a handwritten note lacks manners?" he says. "I object."

"Overruled," I snap. "You're not the one with a mustached criminal currently scaring your cat."

"Scared? The very same cat that let Fiona carry it around all night at a wild Halloween party when it was just a kitten. Alex will take you to my car, where my driver awaits you."

I scoff so hard I choke, coughing into the phone.

"Are you alright? I took a swim this morning. I may have some water in my ear, but you sound like you've swallowed a fur ball."

"You. Are. Infuriating." I look at the mystery man beside me. "Alex? Your cryptic messenger now has a name?"

"He's always had a name. Now go put on something pretty and get in the car."

"Or what?" I hiss into the phone.

His voice drops. "Or I'll come down there myself to retrieve you. And I promise you—you won't like that very much. Get your gorgeous ass in my car. Now."

I let a string of expletives go, calling him every name in the book.

"And madame questions *my* manners." He hangs up.

"Mademoiselle!" I shriek into the phone. I toss it to the side.

I'll go. But only because I need a change of scenery. I can't stay here with Callum's men's eyes on me; I don't want to feel their stares as they question my loyalty.

It would break my already hurting heart.

And honestly, after the explosive fight with Callum in the Great Hall, I knew he was right. He has so much on his plate. I don't want to worry him more.

And after those pain-filled words from my brother outside of O'Malley's...

Freya, how could ye not know?

The words I can't get to stop echoing in my ears. They're weighing me down, breaking my heart repeatedly each time I remember them. A little space between Callum and me could benefit us both.

I'll go, but not for the reason everyone thinks, not to create a relationship with Fredrick.

They say I was too young to remember the moment my parents first laid that precious bundle in my arms. And maybe I was. But if I close my eyes, I can feel Callum's soft, weighted warmth, smell his soft baby scent, and a surge of big sister love and protection fills me.

Callum is a Viking of a man, but he will always be my little brother.

I'll go to protect the one relationship that matters most to me if only to ease my brother's mind. I'll be Freddie's captive if it brings peace to Callum. For now, just until I figure out how to prove to everyone that I am a loyal islander through and through.

But I will NEVER marry him.

And Fredrick best not lay one finger on me.

Or...tongue.

Chapter Eight

F redrick

I HEAD TO THE LIBRARY TO GIVE FREYA A FEW moments to cool off after her funeral performance, pretending to catch up on an unfinished leather-bound classic. I'm halfway through the third chapter when I realize I'm no more knowledgeable on war or peace than when I started. My only focus is Freya.

When locals heard the owner of Frisky Whisky Empire was seeking to staff a large estate home in Inverness, the list of applicants was as long as the river the castle overlooks. I had to choose quickly and asked Sabrina to help. She's spent the last few weeks interviewing her favorites. Little did we know I would be the one taking over the castle and that we needed to staff up immediately.

Sabrina sent me her final group via bus last night. MAWR-vein and her small year-round cleaning crew were prepared for all of us; beds were made in staff rooms, a roaring fire was ready, and electrolyte water was waiting in my enormous owner's suite.

When I first bought Inverness for this plan, I ordered uniforms, hoping to make an excellent first impression on Freya. I was relieved when the Scots Knitwear truck pulled up with the delivery this morning.

MAWR-vein stormed into my office soon after, telling me she would not participate in Inverness's dress code. "Morven, you're far too beautiful to wear a stuffy suit jacket." I pulled out the soft blue apron I ordered for her when I imposed the dress code, a white-stitched emblem of the castle on its pocket.

I could tell by the light in her eyes that she loved the gift in her Morven way; she grumbled as she stomped out of my office, apron already on.

Finally, there's a knock on the library door. I close the book, holding my place with a finger "Enter."

A staff member wearing the khaki blazer with the gold seal of the castle stitched on the breast shows himself. Unlike my housekeeper, Enrique wears his uniform proudly. He looks put together, the blazer giving the young man a boost of confidence.

He greets me with a nod. "Sir. Your guest is settled in the receiving room."

I set the book on the side table while correcting him. "Fiancée."

"Of course. My apologies."

"It's nothing." I stand, following him from the library to the receiving room. "You've been doing great work here today."

He releases a sigh of relief. "Thank you, sir. It was my pleasure to be chosen to come to Inverness."

"Pretty cool living in a castle, no?"

"Yes." He beams a hundred-watt smile, quickly adding, "Sir." He reaches out to grasp the large, black iron handle of the tall, arched door of the receiving room for me, but his fingertips only brush against the metal before the door is thrown open.

The goddess of Freya's namesake, Freyja, is powerful, often depicted as beautiful and alluring, a protector of love, but her role was more complex than that. Having a darker side, she was also the goddess of war. Half of the Norse warriors who died in combat lay in her sacred meadow.

Now, she stands before me in a blaze of her Burnes glory, a bonfire of heat and light, lasers shooting at me from her beautiful green eyes. Her hair has been ripped from her updo and hangs down her back in waves, the lace veil thrown to the floor. Still dressed in her black dress and heels, hands planted on her hips, she stands in the doorway assessing me.

Ready for battle.

I should have gone for the full body armor instead of the swim. "Hello, Freya—"

"Forget the abduction." A hiss of words cuts off my greeting. "What in the Green Hills of Scotland do you think you're playing at, having your driver call me your"—narrowing her eyes, she spits the word out—*"wife?"*

"Abduction?" I look her over. "I see no cuffs, no chains, though you would look lovely in those items. You seem to have come willingly. Of your own accord."

"You're the one who's going to be in chains, buddy. Just wait till Callum finds out about your little circus strongman THREATENING me, telling me to get in the car—"

My time to interrupt her. "Your brother is here."

"What?" Her shocked gaze does nothing to dull her beauty.

"Your brother. Callum. He's here. Now."

"I spoke to him before I answered the door to your henchmen. He's out with Fio—"

"Fiona is here as well."

Grabbing the tiny remote in my pocket, I flick a button. The security monitor over her head comes to life, showing a small gathering of elegantly dressed couples mingling over drinks and hors d'oeuvres in the ballroom.

"What. The. Actual."

"They're eating."

"I can see that they are eating. What I'm wondering is why?"

"Because it's delicious?" Using the laser at the end of the remote, I wave a red circle around the dishes set along the tabletop. "I've ordered all your favorites from your last trip to Paris. Artichoke Helens made by Jaques Pepins himself. Cake d'Alsace—I can see why you love it, that combination of gruyere, bacon, and caramelized onion is delicious—and all flavors of crepes. Wine from my quaint Parisian home. And, of course, sparkling water for me, whisky from our distillery for you and our guests."

Her mouth snaps shut. Then opens. Then closes again.

Finally, she demands, "What are they *doing* here? More importantly, what am *I* doing here? And why is your driver calling me your *wife?*"

"Sit down."

"I'll stand."

"Take," I say, "a seat. You want answers." I pull a chair out, dragging it over the floor. "And I want to review some rules to ensure your safety."

Crossing her arms over her chest, she stares at me, waiting a beat to see what I'll do if she doesn't obey. It's the perfect opportunity to lay down the law and the rules of this estate.

Her safety comes above all else but is the only thing above her comfort. And I'm about to make her very, very uncomfortable.

We remain standing in a face-off which I will win. "Since you don't want to sit, I guess you want to lie down."

"With you?" She gives a haughty laugh as her perfect brow knits. "I don't think so."

I take her hand, and as smoothly as I cut through the icy water of the river, I sit, pulling her over my lap in one fluid motion. In her shock, she has no time to fight me. I swiftly kick my leg around hers, pinning them in place, and wrap an arm around her waist.

Now, she's realizing what's happening. She enters warrior mode, reigniting my wish for full armor. She's wriggling and attempting to kick her way out of my arms like a swimmer herself, but she can't break my hold with her hands pressing into the floor to balance her weight.

She's letting out a long string of unladylike curse words, some of which must be from the island as I've never heard of half of them, ending with, "What in the Highlands do you think you're doing you *durty bag o washin'!*"

I love the feel of her lithe body laid across my lap, helpless and at my mercy. "Your life is in my hands. I'll not tolerate your disobedience."

"You bampot. Scunner. Gleekit—" And on and on.

"Lucky for you, princess, I have no idea what any of those words are, but if you stop your gibberish for a moment, I'll tell you what I'm going to do to you."

She rants until she feels my hand smooth up the backs of her legs, pushing her dress up to her waist. Freezing like an elderberry popsicle, her body tautens as she goes silent, then whispers, "What...are you...doing?"

"Right now? I'm enjoying the lovely sight of your body stretched out over my lap." I smooth my hand over the backs of her bare thighs, sending chill bumps over her skin as I say, "And I'm wondering how I'm going to get these sexy red lace panties down without you kicking me."

"My panties?" She gives a shrill shriek of displeasure. "Well, that will just NOT be happening, aye? I don't know what kind of convoluted agreement you and Callum have come to, but when he hears about this—"

I lean down, asking, "Do you really want to tell your brother that I took you over my lap, pulled down your panties, and spanked you like the naughty girl you are?"

I've rendered her momentarily speechless. I take the opportunity to palm the curve of her ass, cupping her soft skin. "And after I get these pretty panties down, I'm going to punish you." Tucking a finger under the elastic band of her panties where they meet the curve of her hip, I pull them back, letting them go with a snap.

The teasing pop brings her out of her shock.

"Bastard!" Her back arches, and her breath hitches in her throat again.

I cup her ass, pushing my fingers into the soft flesh of her buttocks. "Don't say that again." I can feel her heart racing against my thigh. Knowing that I can reduce my fierce warrior to a shivering, defiant captive in my arms is a powerful feeling.

I grab the back of the band around her waist, tugging.

"Fredrick!" She protests, her strong voice unsteady. "You wouldn't dare."

"Wouldn't I?" I pull down her panties, lining them up under the bottom curve of her ass, taking in another pretty picture of Freya.

Her pale curves are so beautiful, and the ring of red lace that wraps around the tops of her thighs only makes them sexier.

"Do. NOT. Spank me, Fredrick Frisque."

Her words only fuel my determination. With a firm yet gentle hand, I begin to spank her lightly. The sound of flesh meeting flesh fills the air between us, intensifying with each strike until she's squirming and writhing beneath me in protest and arousal. Her pale skin turns light pink under my careful attention.

I give her right cheek a hard spank. "That's one," I say, my voice low and firm. "For not sitting when I asked."

"You have got to be kidding," she seethes.

My hand comes down again, same spot, harder this time, causing her to gasp and arch her back in response. "Two," I continue, my voice a sensual melody against her ears. "For trying to escape my grasp."

My red handprint rises on her flesh, making my cock go hard against her squirming belly. Her breath hitches as my hand descends once more, the force of each spank now leaving a warm imprint across her flesh.

The scent of her arousal fills the air, mingling with the rich scents of our surroundings.

"Three. Now, let's see how wet you are for me." My fingers fight their way between her ass cheeks, slipping into the slick arousal between her thighs. I begin to tease and torment her most sensitive spots. Her body arches, her protests turning into moans as I push the boundaries between pain and pleasure.

My fingers withdraw as I plant another hard spank on her ass. "Four," I say, "for making me want you so badly, my beautiful, feisty Freya."

"Five," I say, my voice a low growl of need as I take in the sight of her reddening ass. "For being so beautiful and tempting that even the strongest part of me can't resist the siren call of your taste."

"This is SO ridiculous! When will this be over!"

"Six," I say, my voice thick with desire. "For your language."

"Seven," I say, spanking her again. "For making me want to keep you locked within these walls forever. To never let you leave my sight."

She moans, twisting in pain, yet the intoxicating scent of her strengthens, filling the room and driving me wild with desire. I want to throw her on the leather sofa and take her now.

But I'm a patient man, and just like whisky aging in an oak barrel, some things are worth waiting for.

"Eight." I spank her on the right cheek. "Nine." The left. "And ten."

I don't tell her the last three are for making me realize I didn't just bring her here for her protection. There's more here between us than me taking her and being satisfied. I've started to wonder if, in some act of insanity, I brought her here because I feel more for her than pure carnal desire.

I lean down to kiss her softly before pulling back and whispering in a low voice, "Are you going to behave now, my little wildcat?"

She moans with defiance before she gives in with a defeated sigh. "Yes," she says through gritted teeth.

Satisfied with her answer, I bring her up, sitting her bare, punished ass on my lap, her panties still around the tops of her thighs. The stiff fabric of her dress stays up around her waist, and I get an enticing peek of her smooth, naked pussy.

"I've brought you here to marry you. Not only will you be safe here away from Glasgow, but our marriage will prove to everyone that you are a King, through and through."

"I can't do that." She shakes her head.

I brush her hair over her shoulder, exposing her neck. "Take your time."

"It would take an eternity—" I cut her off, my lips trailing kisses down her neck, tasting her skin's salty-sweet essence as my hands continue their exploration—until she lets out a low moan.

I pull back slightly, my eyes locking onto her green ones. Her gaze is filled with anger and desire, fury and longing.

I can see the struggle within her, the push-pull of her innate desire to defy me with her overwhelming need for pleasure that only I can provide her.

"Now, I'll have my kiss."

Her eyes fill with shock and desire, and she looks at me, her chest heaving. I lean in, my lips teasing her own, a soft caress that tells her there will be more. Her eyes flutter shut, and she lets out a small moan as I explore her mouth with my tongue, savoring her sweetness.

She kisses me back, and I taste the complexity of emotions on her lips—overwhelmed, angry, but also undeniably hungry. She knows she is at my mercy, yet she can't resist the incredible energy ever-present between us.

She moans softly, pressing into me even more as I continue my exploration. Her skin is warm beneath my hands, flushed and alive with passion.

As I kiss her, I smooth my hand over her body. Although unsure of why she had the reaction she did the other night, I'm careful to avoid her breasts. My hand moves lower, cupping her between her legs and finding her already wet and ready for me. With a slow, torturous pace, I tease and stroke until she's panting and begging for release. My arousal is almost unbearable as I continue to pleasure her.

She writhes and moans beneath my hands, her body surrendering to my touch while her mind fights against it. I can feel my control slipping as I watch her respond to me, every part of her trembling with need.

She breaks away from our kiss, gasping a shaky, "Fredrick," as she tries to catch her breath. She grabs my shoulders, fingers digging into me as she rises into that climax.

"Good girl. Look what you get when you stop fighting me and obey."

Freya breathes out. "I never promised that I would follow your rules."

"You will if you want to come, beautiful girl."

"Mmm..." She gulps, her hips rocking as she chases down that wave of ecstasy.

I push her hair back from her radiant face to take her in. "I want to flip you over right now, spank your ass, punish you again."

"Why?" she gasps.

I bring my lips to her ears, nipping her lobe. "For making me want to fuck you until you no longer remember your name."

Shocked and ready to come, she draws in a tight breath, her entire body tensing as she squeezes her eyes shut tight, clenches her jaw, and throws her head back. I love the feel of her hands on my shoulders, clinging to me, begging me to give her what she needs. I love the heat of her body against me, the smell of her, the sound she makes as she comes, the taste of the curve of her neck as I bite her skin lightly just as she orgasms.

I almost come along with her, the biggest turn-on being the fact that I'm the only man on this earth who can touch her like this, smell her, hear her sounds, and make her come.

The power is intoxicating.

I kiss her again to ease her out of the climax.

She stops me, standing quickly, pulling up her panties and tugging down her dress. She smooths her hair, shaking it free over her back. Locking eyes with me, she says, "Are we finished here?"

The abrupt change from kissing her to her staring daggers at me affects me more than it should. I don't allow it to show; instead, I stand and pull my suit jacket closed over my fading erection.

"Make yourself at home. As long as you stay inside the walls, you are free to explore."

"Fredrick."

"Yes."

"You may make the rules for the estate, but I also make my own rules."

"Is that so," I say.

"Yes. And, aye, I may let you make me come occasionally. But you will never, ever fuck me."

"Madame."

"Are we clear?" she says. "If so, I'm going to find Callum so I can kill him." She turns on her heel to walk out the door.

An empty ache fills my chest. A pain that's not visited me in a very long time. It takes me back home to France, my father's estate, large, cold, and looming. I'm thrust back into that moment in my mother's calming gardens. Standing under that tree. I close my eyes and embrace the pain.

A sense of loss comes over me, so great I want to drag her back over to me and kiss her till she softens in my arms. That desire fights an equally strong sentiment to send her on her way. To not go down this dangerous road. Wanting someone is one thing.

Having them is something else entirely.

Still, I take her arm, stopping her and pulling her back to me. "Your revenge can wait," I say. "Right now, something else takes priority."

One arched brow shoots sky-high as she cocks a hip, pulling her arm from my grasp. "Which would be…"

"We need to get you into your wedding gown."

Chapter Nine

F reya

I GLANCE AROUND THE ROOM I WAS WHISKED TO upon Fredrick's command. A rounded space with exposed stone walls and honey-colored hardwood floors that have been recently refinished. The tall arched windows overlook the pebbled front drive, which is empty, and the car that drove me here is long gone now.

I move to the mirror.

The dress has a high neckline, and sparkling silver beads make a necklace-like halter, drawing attention to my face. The shimmery white gown is entirely backless, dipping low at the waist to show off my slim frame, the fabric flaring into a long, beaded train. The white satin nips just below my ribcage, at the slimmest part of my waist, then flows downward. The skirt has multiple layers of translucent fabric, and hints of glitter sparkle in the light as I move.

It's the most beautiful thing I've ever seen and precisely what I would have chosen for myself, and it fits perfectly.

I stare back at the perfect bride in the mirror.

This wedding gown was designed specifically for me.

But when? And by whom? I think of the delicate artistry of the miniature balloon. Could Fredrick have not only purchased this dress but ordered it to be custom-made too?

A dress like this...would take weeks for a team to make, a solo seamstress, months. My stomach sinks. Am I the disloyal one? I think of Callum's and my fight last night, him reiterating that I needed to leave Norse Garden.

Did he specifically mean to leave home for Inverness? And if so, how long have he and Fredrick been planning my captivity? How far does my brother's heartbreaking disloyalty stretch?

And people say I'm the one betraying the Kings.

The women who spent the last hour silently preparing me, pinning up my long hair, contouring my face with makeup, and dressing me swirl around me, nodding at their work, the crest of the house emblazoned in gold on the lapel of their tan sweater-vests.

At the sound of a knock on the door, they jump to attention, standing with spines straight and hands clasped behind them.

Fredrick appears in the doorway, commanding, "Leave us."

"Stay," I demand, trying to catch the eye of anyone, but all the women's eyes are on him, just as it was in Glasgow whenever Fredrick was in the room.

This time, it's only because he's paying them, I tell myself. Not because of the way his powerful presence fills the room. Or how stunning he looks in the black tux he wears.

I watch him in the mirror. His eyes remain on me as he addresses the room. "Now." One word from Fredrick, they scatter like kitchen roaches when the lights go on at night.

Cowards. If I were to be the lady of the house during my stay, I would get rid of those hideous khaki uniforms they wear and teach these women how to stand up to their boss.

Steeling my nerves, I grit my teeth, turning away from the mirror to face my captor. "Well. I did it. Did you do as you promised?"

He repeats my earlier demands. "Call off the wedding and send the guests away?"

"Yes." I would only agree to wear this dress and stay for dinner if he ended this crazy plan he and my brother concocted.

"Not yet."

"I'm wearing the dress." The white heat of anger creeps over my face. "Why haven't you held up your end of the agreement?"

"I will." He moves closer. Those little hairs on my forearms stand on end, my braless nipples contract, sensitive against the cold sheen of silk. I can smell his cologne, a fragrance I find incredibly sexy, one I would buy for a husband if I had one. If I even wanted one, which I don't. He comes even closer now, light flashing off the face of his handsome watch, putting a shine on his stylish black shoes. "You look amazing."

"So do you," I admit. "If you weren't such a psycho."

A dark-sounding chuckle escapes him. "Psycho? What makes you say that?" His footsteps echo through the empty room as he circles me.

"Um, let's see...arranging a marriage in this day and age. Not informing the wife-to-be, much less asking her consent—"

"Consent is a tricky word for me."

I let the momentary fear this comment instills wash away, remaining stoic as I continue speaking. "Having a dress made to her specifications—I'm guessing since there's no way my friends or Fiona would willingly let this happen to me, you've somehow tapped into my online pinboard for wedding ideas. You shouldn't let that fool you. Every woman has one. Even women like me, ones who never want to marry."

"We'll see." He leans forward, and I will myself not to cringe back. He takes a deep inhale.

"Are you...smelling me?"

"Yes. Amazing. You smell as good as you look."

"See. Psycho. Path."

"I know you taste even better than you smell." His eyes lock on mine, and something in his dark, confident gaze sends a shock of electricity bolting to my core. "Wife-to-be."

"Och, hell no. Let's stop with all that nonsense right now. I may have agreed to dinner, but I certainly—"

"Have you agreed to dessert?"

The word dessert grabs my attention enough to stop my monologue. "Huh?"

Now his hand is on my waist, slipping over the silk, heat and control where there was nothing. My usual stilettos were traded for ballet slippers; he's much taller than me as he stares down at my face. "Do you agree to dessert?"

Is this a trick question? Who wouldn't agree to dessert?

I'm trying to figure out how to answer him. I live for sweets, but the question is part of his game. There's no way he's got one of those uniformed women hiding behind the Chinese dressing screen, ready to roll out a cart of cake slices from Sugar Rush on Byres Street.

Does he?

I do adore wedding cake.

Before I can decide what to say, he's wrapping his body around mine, his arms encircling me, his warm hands pressing against my bare back. "I have a treat in mind."

"Is it chocolate?" I ask.

"No."

"More evidence you're trying to marry the wrong woman," I say.

"You don't want to know what I have in mind?" A smoldering grin covers his face as he glances down at my very pert nipples in the gown.

"I'm not sure I do."

His hands run down the sides of my body, and I do nothing to stop them. He drops to one knee, staring up at me as if to propose. "I'm having a craving," he says, gently moving the tulle of my skirt away from my body. "For my dessert."

Before I can blink, the man is buried under the many gauzy layers of the wedding dress, his hands stroking my bare legs, grazing up my thighs, and hooking into the waistband of the white silk thong I wear. He drags the material down my legs, dropping them around my ankles.

My hands don't know what to do as I sputter in shock. "What—what are you trying to do?" I feel hot breath on the bare skin of my smooth pussy, strong hands wrapping around the backs of my thighs.

"Oh. God. Oh my God." The slick heat of his tongue darts out, licking my pussy, the soft tip wriggling and tickling my clit. A tight little orgasm immediately breaks free from me as my body gives an involuntary, hard shudder.

"I want something else from you. For making me cancel our beautiful wedding." He's angry, frustrated, and tired of getting me off while being left hard and cold. "The gown isn't enough."

He wants to own me, control me, dominate me. And he wants my pretty lips wrapped around his cock. Proving my point, he stands up and backs away, his hand going to the buckle of his belt.

"Careful what you wish for," I say.

"Why? Do you bite as well as bark?"

"Are you calling me a dog?"

"Are you threatening me?"

"No, only warning you."

"Warning me about your fellatio?" he snaps. "Are you that bad at it?"

"No. I'm that good."

He doesn't say anything, just stares, the look in his gaze turning to pure hunger.

"Once you've had my mouth wrapped around your cock, you won't be able to think of anything else."

He swallows a tight lump in his throat. "I'll take my chances."

I'm not shitting him. Islander girls are known for being good girls, maintaining their precious virginity as long as possible, but we still love our men. I may be inexperienced in other areas, but I'm damn good at pleasing a man with my mouth.

Him being helpless under my seduction will be a welcome power exchange

'Cause even though I'll be the one on my knees, he'll be entirely at my mercy.

"And no," I add. "I don't bite."

Often.

Hips rolling, I stride over to him, flattening my palm against the center of his chest. Holding his gaze, I push him backward until he falls onto the bed and sits on the edge.

He's staring up at me for once.

I stand over him, Freya Warrior Princess, ready to go into battle.

"I'm going to make you weak. Make you beg for mercy." Placing my hands on his knees, I lean forward, close enough to kiss him. "You're going to be begging me to let you come."

"Let me come?"

"Allow you to, if and when I choose." I brush my lips over his. When he tries to kiss me, I pull back.

"A sliver of power," he murmurs, "and she goes crazy."

"Crazy? You're the one who's about to lose your mind." I sink to my knees, making him hold my gaze as I slowly unbuckle that leather belt of his, letting my fingers brush over his already-growing erection.

His eyes burn into mine, the hunger and desire reflected in their depths mirroring my own. The tension between us is palpable, the air thick with anticipation as I finally free his erection from his pants, lightly dragging the backs of my knuckles along his stiff shaft. He gasps softly.

I wrap my hand around his shaft, slowly stroking it as I gaze into his eyes. He lets out a low groan at my touch. The power I have over him is almost intoxicating; he's so eager, so desperate for me, while I can take my time, savoring the moment.

"Please." His hands go behind him as he leans back, thrusting his hips up, needing me to take him in my mouth.

"I haven't even begun, and you're already begging."

He swallows hard, his deep brown eyes searching mine, trying to read my intentions. He has beautiful eyes, something I'd never noticed before given their usual hard expression. Now, with his wanting me so badly, I almost feel connected to him in his need.

Drunk on power, I push the thought away, letting Dominatrix Freya out to play.

I lean in closer, my breath warm against his skin as I continue to stroke him. I can feel the tension in his muscles, the way he's holding himself back. But not for long.

"I'm going to free you from this prison," I say softly, my fingers moving faster now, teasing the sensitive skin of his cock with a quick lash of the tip of my tongue. "Even as you hold me captive in yours."

His breath hitches, his body trembling slightly with desire and anticipation. He lets out a low growl, lunging forward, his hands gripping my shoulders tightly as I continue to stroke him, his hips moving instinctively to meet my hand.

"You want to be free?" he asks hoarsely, his eyes locking onto mine with a raw intensity that makes my stomach flutter. "To not be locked away, caged in by these walls and rules and me? Or do you want to live?"

His words strike fear into my heart, remembering the self-inflicted danger that brought me here in the first place. Frustrated with myself, I take it out on his cock.

The head of his cock tastes salty and sweet, the skin warm and firm beneath my tongue. I stroke him slowly, taking him deeper into my mouth as I savor the feel of him against my lips.

The veins in his shaft are throbbing, a testament to his arousal. I increase the pace of my strokes, my hand moving up and down his length with reckless abandon. My mouth moves in tandem, sucking and slurping at his head as I tease and tantalize.

I glance up at him. The sight of him losing control is almost too much for me to bear; his eyes are wide and glassy, his lips parted slightly as he pants for air. His chest rises and falls rapidly, each breath sending another wave of arousal through him.

"Fuck...yes," he groans, unable to hold back any longer. It's music to my ears; I want him to lose control, to let go and surrender to me. "Fuuuuuck." He thrusts upward as I suck and stroke him. Releasing my shoulders, he leans back, his hands tight around the bedding, covers shifting as he grips them.

I smile around him, feeling powerful and in control.

His hands release the covers and reach for me, tighten in my hair, guiding me as I bob my head up and down his shaft. The pulsing of his cock throbs against my lips. He smells and tastes of man and desire, intoxicating and irresistible.

He moans loudly, his hips bucking involuntarily as I explore every inch of him with my mouth. He moans my name. "Freya. God, Freya. You're incredible." His words are a victory cry for me.

He's desperate for release.

I pull back, my eyes locked with his as I continue to stroke him gently. "Tell me how good I am," I whisper, my voice a seductive purr. "Tell me how much you want me."

He swallows hard, his eyes wide and wild with desire. "You're the sexiest thing I've ever seen," he gasps out, his breath ragged with his fight against the urge to come. "Your mouth, your tongue, your lips. There is no woman like you, Freya."

The sincerity in his words almost brings me to a pause. I slide my lips over the head of his cock, a satisfied grin spreading across my face as he twitches against my mouth. Almost folding in half at the waist, he groans, his hands tangling in my hair as he tries to control himself. I savor the taste of him, the salty sweetness of his arousal, taking him deeper into my mouth.

His hips buck wildly beneath me, thrusting upward, and he comes. I feel the warmth of his release flood my mouth, the taste of him suddenly sweeter and more intense. I savor it for a moment before swallowing, a small smile playing on my lips.

"Perfect," I murmur, pulling away and leaning down to kiss the sensitive tip. He lets out a shuddering breath, his eyes still wide with a mix of pleasure and shock.

I straighten up and look at him, my eyes locking with his. "You're not the only one in charge here at Inverness." I stand up, my body glowing with the power of dominance.

He stares at me, his gaze heavy with desire and a hint of fear. He knows he's been bested and is no match for me in this game. And yet, something in his eyes tells me he doesn't mind, that he even craves it, too.

"You're crazy," he says finally, his voice hoarse and laden with a mixture of lust and admiration. He reaches out and runs his fingers along my waist, like he wants to grab me and pull me in for a kiss, his touch sending a thrill through me.

"Maybe," I say, meeting his gaze head-on. "But you keep underestimating me."

He chuckles, a low and deep sound that leaves me wet. "I don't think I'm underestimating you. I think I'm the only man who really knows you. And I think you love the chase."

His words hit me in the center of my chest, take my breath, then anger rises. We've only been together a few times. How could he have the audacity to say something like that?

A nagging thought pricks at me; the truth is what upsets us most. Could he be right? I hide the smile that wants to creep onto my lips. "Well, keep chasing then," I say, turning away from him and walking to the door.

As I step out of the room, I can feel his eyes on me, watching my every move. It's an intoxicating feeling, knowing that I have control over him. And yet, there's a part of me that craves his dominance.

My wild nature and free spirit lean toward the dominance he delivers. Every ounce of me screams for him to take control, command, and make me obey. And he's right; I crave the chase.

He knows me too well. And I think I hate him for it.

Chapter Ten

F reya

THE CASTLE IS A STURDY TWO-STORY RED sandstone square sandwiched between three towers. All the windows are arched at the top in half-moons, and when you stand inside the towers you can peer out the windows there for a lovely view of the river.

It's a beautiful land. A dream of a wee little castle. It is the perfect renovation project. A home to house generations of frisky little Frisques. And those brown-eyed French-speaking weapons will not be popping out of this golden minge.

But the way Fredrick is following me so closely, at my side every moment of the day, I'm near afraid I'll get pregnant merely from spending too much time alone with the man.

"It's a gorgeous estate," I say. "I'd love to tour it in peace."

"You mean alone?"

"Aye."

"No." My tour guide and I stand out on the pebbled path where I first arrived, staring up at the castle as he informs me, "Built in the late 1800s, the estate home lovingly nicknamed Wee Inverness was modeled after the original Inverness castle, which was the fictional home of the infamous Lady Macbeth."

"Lady Macbeth! That's fascinating."

"As the lady of the house, you will now be our Lady Macbeth."

"I'm not the lady of the house. Only a guest." A temporary one at that. "And please do not compare me to a power-hungry manipulative woman who plans a murder and then encourages her husband to carry it out for her." I toss my hair over my shoulder. "Obviously, I'd carry out my own murders."

"Hypothetically?" he hopes.

I pull down my white-framed Chanel sunglasses to peek at him in warning. "Don't push me."

"I only meant Lady Macbeth is strong, ambitious"—he chokes out the last word—"ruthless." Clearly thinking of me on my knees. I laugh, picturing him on the edge of the bed last night, gripping the sheets and groaning out eff bombs as I pleasured him.

"Back to my request for the solo tour. Last night, when you first came in the room and were—" I flush, ashamed about laying over his lap.

"Spanking you and punishing you. Turning you on?" he says.

Clearing my throat, I ignore him, continuing, "You told me that I could go anywhere I wanted as long as I stayed within the walls." I hold up a gold-bangled wrist, pointing to the tall stone wall surrounding the property. "I'm within the wall, ken?"

"I said you could explore inside the walls, yes."

"And?"

"I never said you could go alone."

Infuriated, I moan. "Semantics."

"You're a lawyer." He shrugs. "You know how important it is to pay attention to the details."

I heave a sigh. "I am a lawyer, and this whole 'no contact with the outside world' thing is driving me bananas! I mean, I know we just wrapped up two cases, and it's the perfect time to have a"—I hold up my fresh red manicure to air quote—"vacation, but seriously. I'm a CONTROL freak. Not having any idea how work is going..."

"It's for your safety," he reminds me for the numpty-teenth time. "As well as that of your friends. If the Hoax came looking for you, whoever is around you at the time could be hurt."

"I agree. It's just frustrating. You know—you don't have to babysit me. Don't you have your own work to do?"

"I could use a vacation. Besides, if I don't babysit you, who's going to spank that lovely ass of yours if you get out of hand?"

HEAT. Everywhere. "Have I told you how infuriating I find you?"

He counters with, "Have I told you how enchanting I find *you?*"

My entire wardrobe arrived this morning. I must say, I am looking good. I'm opting for a French flair for my first day as the MAD-mo-zelle of the castle. I wear a light, cashmere blue-and-white-striped sweater. I teamed it with fitted white pants, nude thong panties underneath, and Kate Spade kitten-heeled slingbacks on my feet. I completed the outfit with a lovely straw hat to keep the warm, late-fall sun from my face, a blue ribbon around its brim.

"I've never seen you in anything other than black." He adds, "Or purple. Or naked."

The cheek! "You've never seen me naked," I correct.

"I've seen parts of your stunning body naked. Your thighs, your—"

"Let me stop you right there." I change to a safer subject, my outfit. "I shocked myself this morning when I chose this outfit, but I woke up feeling..."

Free is the word I want to use, but that would make absolutely no sense. Banished from my home, I'm a captive here. Yet, having some space from Callum and the Kings, I feel free.

"Ready to conquer the day?"

"Exactly," I say. "And the idea of wearing black made me miss the courtroom that much more."

"Hopefully, you won't find staying at our little castle too terrible a time."

"You've been more than generous," I offer. "And, so far," fingers crossed, "I'm not hating it as much as I anticipated when your circus hand dragged me away from my cozy home."

He clears his throat, hiding a laugh.

SHOCKER: I am having a lovely time. Last night's sexcapades didn't hurt either. I was Freya, the sexy Valkyrie, and I conquered the stuffy French man, rocking his privileged world, showing him what we simple islanders are made of. We don't need prestigious boarding schools for a good education.

A few drinks, a good bonfire night, and a grassy hill with privacy will teach you everything you need to know to rule this man's world.

Of course, a few years of law school didn't hurt either.

"Come this way," he says, leading me toward a lovely gazebo at the water's edge. The scent of fresh coffee hits my nose, making it a wee bit easier to follow behind him.

"I've had the staff prepare a breakfast picnic for us."

"Fredrick, you really don't have to spoil me," I say, loving the attention. After Callum's betrayal, I'm licking my wounds. A little thoughtfulness goes a long way in recovering my former confidence.

"Smoked salmon, caviar, and liver paté. French delicacies."

"Oh." I smooth a false brightness to my tone. "Lovely!"

What I could use this morning is a deep-fried Mars bar.

Still, I behave, following him to a table by the water. It is nice to know someone cares. The river sparkles under the sun, and the little town stretching out on the other side of the water is pristine and quaint.

The table is filled with fresh coffee and sweets.

"Wait a minute, you tricky trickster. These are what Fiona calls my Freya foods." Mini powered doughnuts. Raspberry ruffle bars. Tea cakes.

"I've told you, I want you to be comfortable here. Anything your little Freya heart desires, say the word, and you shall have it." He gestures at the table. "Please, dive in."

"If you insist." I pick up a ruffle bar and take a delicate bite. The delicious taste confirms what I suspected. "I'd know this Raspberry Ruffle anywhere. This is Cheffie's recipe!"

He nods. "I didn't want you homesick, so I asked Cheffie to send some of your favorites along with your wardrobe.

"That was very thoughtful of you." My heart does this weird fluttering thing. He reached out to Cheffie just for me? Feeling I owe him thanks, I stretch up, landing a chaste kiss on his cheek. His intoxicating masculine scent has me pulling back quickly. "Thank you."

"It's nothing. Truly." He reaches over, picking up a frosty glass. "Your favorite flavor of fruit smoothie with added protein powder for your health."

He hands me the glass, and I accept, taking a deep drink. "Delicious. Thank you. You've thought of everything."

He dines on the fresh fruit and cheese platter while I sample every dessert, thinking it would be rude not to after all the thought he's put into our picnic.

I hold out my glass. "Smoothie?" I offer.

"No thanks. The French prefer to chew our food."

Conversation flows between us. Witty banter is a must for me, and I have to admit, the man delivers. The weather is unseasonably warm, and under the shining sun and the river's sparkle, I almost feel I'm dining on the French Riviera with a man I much like.

Strange how after all our filthy sexcapades and the electric sexual tension between us, we can transition to having a pleasant day out.

I'm almost enjoying myself when he ruins the mood with, "The wedding. Have you given it more thought?"

I pop a grape into my mouth, enjoying the burst of flavor. "Not a chance. I don't have a plan. I don't know how long I'll be here, how I'll sort out this mess I've made, but I will." I give him a pointed look. "And I won't need a husband to accomplish the task. I'm no weak woman."

"Quite the opposite," he says, admiring my face in the sun. "Which is why you'd make the perfect mafia wife."

"One day. Perhaps. If I meet the right man," I admit.

He looks around; seeing no other men to choose from, he points to himself, saying, "Moi?"

I almost laugh. "No-*wa*," I rhyme with moi, "and no way." I shake my head, the silk ribbon from my hat brushing over my back. "There's too much...tension...between us."

"But you like the fight as much as you like the chase, ma chérie." He slips a hand along my face, cupping my cheek in that lovely way that only he's ever done. He pulls me in for a kiss.

And I let him.

The kiss has sparkle and magic and lingers on my lips. His taste is clean and manly, and I now know firsthand why they call it French kissing. He's a god at it. He holds my face as he kisses me, then lets me go.

Too soon.

I pull away, flushed and bothered. Shaken, I stand, smoothing my pants. "Shall we continue our tour?" I leave the pavilion, getting a few meters head start to cool off.

"Wrong direction."

"Eh?" I look over my shoulder at him.

He points to the other side of the property, away from where I'm headed. "We're going to the gardens."

I catch up to him, taking his arm, and we stroll to the walled gardens behind the castle. We don't get to explore them, though, because there's a line of sleek, shiny, brand-new sports cars parked on the stone patio before the garden, blocking our path.

"Fredrick," I say. "Is there a car show in town?"

"I thought you might like having a car here in Inverness. To drive around the property, of course," he adds. "Pick whichever one you want. The others I'll return."

"I've never owned a car," I say in shock.

"Freya Burnes? Big shot lawyer, no car?"

"No car. In fact—" He's going to have a flippin' field day with this one. "I never learned to drive one."

"How old are you again?"

"Eh? Twenty-and-none-of-your-business years young," I snap. "We didn't need a car on the island—we weren't allowed to go anywhere the bus couldn't take us. Then, Callum and the Kings were in Glasgow, now wealthy and buying bikes and cars. He always drove me to university. Besides messing around and driving Baynes's Toyota truck on the farm, I've never driven."

"Pick one." His gaze scans the line of shiny new cars. "I'll teach you."

I picture the two of us in the red Ferrari, him trying to explain the mechanics to me, me running us off the road, us arguing all the while. "Och," I laugh. "That'll go over well."

If my non-existent driving skills don't do us in, we'll probably end up killing one another anyway.

"You think we can't work together well enough to maneuver a car? How are we to run an estate together once you're my wife?"

"Easy. I'm nae going to be your wife."

"Madam." The easy grin creeps over his face. He's so sure of himself, confident he will be my future husband.

I go to correct him. "It's MAD—you know what? Never mind."

"We will be married. Mrs. Freya Frisque. Has a nice sound, oui?"

"No!" Gah! "You are infuriating. And Freya Frisque, while having a lovely alliteration, is only a fantasy in your extremely addled brain."

I storm away before I even get to fight with him from behind the wheel of one of the lovely vehicles, calling over my shoulder, "And the cars, while lovely, will not change my mind."

And, of course, he follows me.

How we've gone so quickly from our peaceful picnic to this is precisely why we are not a match. "Freaky Freddie the stalker," I murmur to myself, struggling through the grass as I aerate the lawn with the sharp points of my heels.

He rushes to my side, slipping an arm into mine. I would reject it, but the alternative is slipping the heels off and going barefoot, and that's not the look I'm going for. I allow him to assist me to the paved walkway.

"We still need to tour the wine cellars and the horse barns; you haven't even met Joyeux Halloween," he says.

At the word Halloween, I stop in my tracks, turning to face him. "Did you just say Happy Halloween in French?"

"Oui. Or, aye." He grins. "My Joyeux."

"Who," I add, remembering the wee bit of French I learned in Paris, "or what, is your Happy Halloween?"

"Mon chat." His tone fills with adoration. "My kitty."

My jaw drops. "You have a cat?"

"I do. He rode all the way here from Glasgow right in my lap. Unfortunately, Morvan has horrid allergies, and she's banished him to the barns. She says everyone at Inverness has a job, and Joyeux's job is to catch mice. I don't have the heart to tell her he's no mouser and that the only gift he's ever left on my doorstep was a moth."

"He sounds like a sweetie." The man I found so infuriating

a moment ago now tugs my heartstrings. "Halloween...so he's all black?"

"Yes. Well, no. He has a tiny white fur bow tie just here." He runs a finger along the hollow at the base of my neck. My skin responds with a trail of heat in the wake of his touch. "Other than that, he's your favorite color of couture: midnight black."

"He sounds very handsome."

The quaint barn is painted a soft brown with white trim and large windows, a place you could host a rustic wedding.

Fredrick calls the cat's name once. A moment later, a black streak is running right toward him. He scoops up the tiny cat, holding him in the crook of his arm as he tells me how, on a stormy night in Glasgow, he was taking his trash down to the bin behind his apartment above the distillery—he takes out his own trash?—and heard a distressed meow coming from the street.

In the pouring rain, he got down on his belly, reached into a storm drain where he heard more meows, and coaxed the little kitten into his hands.

Happy Halloween is obsessed with the man. Like Ginger, he wants NOTHING to do with yours truly. Seeing Fredrick so tender, caring for the helpless little kitten, knowing he had no parental love to mimic? The gentle display gives me a few healthy throbs in my uterus.

"I like your cat." I press my thighs together, telling my minge to shush. "You know I have a soft spot for All Hallows Eve."

"I'm aware."

"I really like his name. I'm just surprised you would choose something so...fun." I stare at the adorable kitten. "I'm thinking, Cat. Maybe Mr. Cat. Or if you were feeling frisky, perhaps Midnight?"

"You don't think I'm fun?" he asks, bemused.

"You've spent the first half of the morning rattling off dates and facts about the history of the town of Inverness."

Flashing a wicked grin. "You find me quite amusing when I'm under your skirts."

"Och. Boy."

"Here's a fun fact," he says. "Did you know the name Frisky Whisky was because I lost a bet? My friend knew I would hate it, so he bet me twenty grand in a card game. If I won, I got the cash. If he won, he got to name my brand."

"I can see why you wouldn't have wanted that name," I say. "Not a fun fact, though. Not as fun as naming your cat after my favorite holiday."

"I know it's your favorite—I've been to your party. Twice." He grins. "I especially like the taste of the dessert I stole at the last one."

I blush. "You're mad."

"Top three?" he asks.

I raise my brows. "Holidays?"

He nods, nuzzling his cheek against the cat.

"I think you can guess my number one. Then Christmas. I go over the top at Norse Garden. Fresh greenery, red bows, about ten thousand strings of white lights. You should see it." I go quiet momentarily, realizing this mess may not be cleared up by then. "Anyway. And number three, being a loyal Scot, St. Andy's Day."

"Ah—St. Andrew's Day, the feast of the Apostle Andrew," he confirms.

"The very same. Also lovingly referred to as St. Andy's for a beloved tennis player of ours—you know what? Never mind. You can call it whatever you like as long as you partake in the festivities."

"Years ago, I arrived in Scotland for the first time on November thirtieth. That was quite an experience."

I try to picture Fredrick in his dark gray suits and perfect manners, trying to navigate sidewalks filled with inebriated Scots. The image tickles me with a giggle.

"On behalf of Scotland, I do apologize. Every Scot you bumped into was probably dead blootered," I laugh. "We go to church, of course, but after service, St. Andy's Day is an excuse to get wreaked and stuff ourselves silly with our beloved traditional foods."

"For you that means mounds of sweets and pounds of crumbly tablet, which I quickly learned not to call fudge."

"I eat sausage!" Happy Halloween looks up at me, and I take the opportunity to reach out and let the little cat sniff me. He seems content enough with my presence, so I stroke him under his silky chin. He doesn't seem to mind.

My fingers brush against Fredrick's skin as I pet the kitten. He doesn't seem to mind, either. I ask him, "What's your favorite holiday?"

"Oh. Hmm." His voice drops. "Honestly, holidays for me

are a bit like driving for you. I don't have much experience in celebrating them."

The thought of not celebrating holidays hits me square in the chest. It's unthinkable. "Like, any of them?"

He shakes his head.

Aghast, I pry further. "What about birthdays?"

"My father didn't believe in frivolous—his words, not mine—silly sentiments. He saw celebrations as time wasters."

That's cold. Ice cold. Island waters in the dead of winter cold. "And your ma? Did she not wish ye a happy birthday?"

"No." He shakes his head. "Not that I remember of her anyway. She died when I was young."

Gah! "I've put my foot in it, haven't I?"

"No, it's just truth. It's what happened. My mother died. My father realized a child wasn't a tiny adult. He didn't know what to do with me. I was shipped off to boarding school at a very young age. Not a lot to celebrate, unfortunately."

"Would you like to celebrate holidays? You have your own grand house now. You can host half of Glasgow here."

"I'd need a wife for that. Wouldn't I?" He turns those deep brown eyes on me. While holding a kitten.

I shake my head. "Don't look at me like that."

"You looked phenomenal in that wedding dress." He leans over so Happy Halloween can jump down. The cat rubs his ankles. "Let's not waste such a gorgeous gown."

Ah. The dress. The one that would have had to be ordered weeks ago.

"It's lovely," I agree. "The loveliest I've ever seen. And it fits me like a glove. Sheer perfection."

"You are sheer perfection. The dress is just a bow on a perfect package."

"Pretty words, but they bring up a pertinent question."

Happy's green eyes and Fredricks's brown eyes stare at me in unison. "Which is?"

"You only brought me here yesterday. A dress like that? Hmmm." I look up at the blue sky as if calculating days. "It takes some time, aye?"

Realization settles uncomfortably on his face.

I narrow my gaze, going in for the kill. "Who ordered the dress, and when?"

He runs a hand over the back of his neck. "I fear I'm not at liberty to say."

"It's Callum. Isn't it?" Hands go to my hips. "He didn't just fear for me after the court case. He's been planning this forever."

He doesn't answer. His gaze says it all. Callum and he had been planning this way before I represented Jack Maclean.

I give a low moan of frustration. Happy meows. Fredrick sighs.

Callum's not trying to save me. He's trying to get rid of me. The realization hits hard.

Awkwardly, I say, "Thanks for letting me meet your sweet kitty. I'll head to the house for a bit to warm up." I leave the barn, rushing toward the castle for the solace of my room before the tears come.

Since Fiona moved in with us and christened our place Norse Garden Estate, I thought things were even better than when it was just Callum and me, as if he had gained a wife and me, a sister.

I likened us to the three musketeers.

Maybe I've had it all wrong.

Maybe…three is a crowd.

Chapter Eleven

F redrick

THE NEXT FEW WEEKS ARE A FLURRY OF ACTIVITY. I know her heart aches for her family, and I want to keep her as distracted as possible as Callum works to make amends with the islander Kings while planning an act of retribution against the Hoax for using Freya as they did.

And if he can't?

Our marriage must go forward. She'll need that extra layer of protection. Until then, I'll do everything I can to keep her safe.

Though my current job for the Kings is much less tumultuous than Callum's, I dare say my days are filled with more tension than his. The constant pull and tug of power between Freya and me, the sexual tension notwithstanding, has me on my toes every moment of every day with her.

No matter how things work out for Freya, I'm determined to make her my wife. Defeating the Hoax feels like a chess game compared to getting the fiery Valkyrie princess to marry me. I've not given up hope.

The dress remains hung in her closet, where she can see it daily. Every morning, she moves it to a different closet in the castle. I seek it out every afternoon, replacing it in her closet so it's there when she prepares for our evening meal together.

If Joyeux and I get my way, one of these nights, she will wear it again.

Days are spent walking the property, planning renovation projects, and training the young staff.

We work well together.

Except when we don't.

Nights, we dine together in the dining room, dressed well, having "good banter" as she says, her sipping wine or whisky, me sparkling water. We make a pretty picture. After our meal, I walk her to her room. She allows me a kiss. Then sends me to bed in my separate room.

With tension in my balls that makes me feel as if they'll break, I've taken to swimming in the nude at night, under the moonlight, the frigid temperatures cooling my blood. MAWR-vein stands on the river's edge, blankets wrapped around her shoulders.

"Lifeguarding" me, as she says. There's no way she'd go in after me, but she figures she can call for help. I think she's softening toward me. The luxury suite I booked in town for her and her husband to celebrate St. Andrews's Day probably didn't hurt our relationship.

She's not taken to Freya like I'd hoped.

"Too pretty," she said to me. "The pretty ones are nothing but trouble, Mr. Fredrick."

Luckily, I'm game for a bit of trouble where Freya is concerned.

Tomorrow is St. Andrews Day, and as Freya says, it's a big deal in Scotland. It happens every year on November thirtieth and celebrates a saint named Andrew, who was once an apostle. In 1320, he became the official patron saint of Scotland when they declared they wanted to be their own independent country.

Hourrah Scotland!

See. I can be fun.

The day is all about having a good time and embracing Scottish culture—that means tables spread with food, lots of fiddles and bagpipes, and Scots debuting their best moves on the dance floor, ceilidh dancing into the late hours of the night.

And they eat, God, they eat.

For starters, there's Cullen Skink soup—the soup tastes better than the name sounds—made with smoked haddock, taters, as they call the potato, and onions. Then comes the main course: haggis (if you're brave enough), turnips, and mashed potatoes. You can make it at home or go to any pub or restaurant in Scotland that day for the classic options. For dessert, warm up with some clootie dumplings and custard—a delicate Scottish dish with dried fruit, spices, oats or breadcrumbs, flour, and beef suet. I've no idea, nor do I want to know, the meaning of the word clootie.

It's a bank holiday. MAWR-vein threatened to lead the staff in a revolt if I didn't give them St. Andrews Day off with pay. As I had already planned, I gave them the day off with pay and threw in a generous bonus with a note telling them their St. Andy's Day drinks are on me.

MAWR-vein truly has a husband, a reclusive artist who lives in a cabin in the forest. Tonight, they have a date planned at their favorite pub, The Walrus and the Carpenter, where they will enjoy buckets of ale and piles of haggis.

With the staff away and neither of us allowed to use the stove—they didn't teach a cooking class in the fancy boarding school I attended—I planned a getaway evening for Freya and me.

There will be no party, no rowdy pub for her this year. I need to distract her from that fact, so I'm taking her into town. I'll have the place we're going heavily guarded and escorts for the drive. She'll be safe outside my walls from the Hoax for this one night.

She won't be safe from me, though.

I'm taking her to the private sex club in Inverness to have my way with her. I want to show her that I am fun and have a wild side, even if it differs from hers. I don't drink. Don't dance. But I know how to show a woman a good time.

Of course, me being me, I'd already pre-arranged the room we'd be using, and before they left for their St. Andy's Day parties, I sent my staff to clean, disinfect, and provide me with implements from my own home.

See?

Good clean fun.

We enter the underground club to the thrum of fast-paced music, the scent of sex mingled with sandalwood.

Freya looks radiant in the dim lighting, her blonde hair dancing around her shoulders, illuminated by the flickering lights and lasers. She's chosen a bright red, sleeveless minidress that hugs her body, lipstick in a matching red. Her pale skin glows with a natural radiance, her classic beauty turning heads as we walk in.

As we make our way through the crowd, I can't help but notice the reactions from the other patrons. They clearly understand that Freya is not just another woman to be admired but a goddess among mere mortals. It's intoxicating to be seen with her, as if you gain status as a man just by being seen with her.

I take her hand in mine, feeling the warmth of her skin and the pulsing energy that seems to emanate from her very being. She looks up at me, her eyes wide and curious. "I don't know if I can do this."

"I thought I was the stuffy one," I tease.

Her eyes dart around the club as she takes in the crowd. "I've...um...I've never done anything like this."

"Ready for an adventure?" I ask, my voice a low murmur.

She looks at me with fear and excitement. A smile slowly creeps onto her face as she squeezes my hand and nods. "Let's do it," she says, her voice barely above a whisper.

We make our way to the heart of the crowd, the pulsating music getting louder and more intense as we approach. The energy is palpable, the rhythm of the music fueling the bodies that sway and grind against each other.

I guide Freya toward a dark corner, away from the main dance floor. I press her against the wall, my body crashing against hers. "Are you sure about this?" I ask, my lips brushing against her ear.

"I trust you," she says, clutching onto my shirt.

I pull her closer, our bodies pressed against each other, every inch of her soft and warm against my touch. Heat radiates from her body, along with her nervous energy, her arousal.

I don't dance but I've been told I kiss like a god.

I press my mouth to hers. It's like an electric current flowing through us both. She melts into the kiss, her fingers clutching my shirt as if she wants to pull me even closer, her long nails brushing against my skin. She murmurs into my mouth, "God damn, you know how to make a girl's knees go weak."

The woman can rule a courtroom, a place where I'm sure I'd clam up. Here, in the club, my blood heats, my curiosity piqued. She's out of her element. She needs me. I feel myself getting lost in the music and the rhythm of our tongues. The music and energy connect us on a deeper level.

I break our kiss to lock eyes with her, the intensity of the need in her gaze making my heart race. For a moment, we stand there, lost in each other's gaze, our bodies still pressed against each other. We're in our own world in the corner of the crowded club.

Finally, I say, "Are you ready to enter a room?"

"I don't know," she admits. "What's in the rooms?"

"Depends on what you choose."

"What are the options?" she asks.

"One, two or three," I say.

"You want me to choose?" she squeaks.

"Yes." I run the pad of my thumb over her bottom lip. "You seal your own fate."

I love the look of trust in her eyes as she stares up at me. "And I don't get to know what's behind the door before I choose?"

I lean in, nipping her earlobe. "Now, what would be the fun in that, princess?"

"Fine." She takes a shaky breath. "I choose...one."

We make our way to the sex room that I had earlier prepared for us tonight. I told a tiny white lie to keep her safe tonight; this is room one, two, and three. It's decorated in black velvet and wood, creating an atmosphere of luxury and sophistication. As she enters, I can see the apprehension in her eyes and her deep curiosity.

Candles burning in a candelabra over our heads cast a warm glow on the walls, and black velvet covers every surface. The air is filled with an intriguing mix of exotic perfumes; I catch a hint of orange and sandalwood.

Freya stops moving into the room as she spots the chains that hang from the ceiling, fur-lined handcuffs dangling from them. The metal chains and cuffs starkly contrast with the luxurious setting. They also symbolize trust and submission, heating my blood with anticipation.

I don't like games, but with her, I'll always play.

Grabbing her hand, I pull her to the center of the room. I snag the cuffs, removing them from the chains. My voice is a rake over hot coals. "Are you ready?"

She nods, her eyes on other chains that hang from the wall. Slowly, she holds out her hands to me, silver fingernails glittering, her eyes full of angst yet anticipation. I take her wrists, kissing them in turn before fastening a cuff around each one.

Raising her cuffed wrists over her head, I adjust the length of the ceiling chains and fasten them securely to the cuffs.

"Do you trust me?" I ask, my voice a low murmur.

She looks up at me, a jumble of emotions. She glances down at her breasts as if she wants to remind me not to touch them. Instead, she glances back at me, saying, "I do trust you."

"Thank you." I begin to explore every inch of her body—carefully avoiding her chest—my hands running down her back, over her sides, her stomach. Every touch is deliberate, every movement calculated to create a wave of pleasure and anticipation in her.

Arms reaching high, her short dress has ridden up. I reach lower, my hands brushing against the sensitive skin of her naked inner thighs. She lets out a small gasp. Her breathing becomes ragged, her eyes shining, her cheeks flushed in the candlelight.

"I'm not stuffy. I'm calculated. But I do enjoy some games." I reach for the riding crop on the wall, flicking it before her. "Ready to play?"

Freya's eyes widen as I hold up the crop. She's both apprehensive and intrigued by what this new element might bring. She steels her nerves, narrowing her gaze. "Of course," she says, her voice shaky but determined.

I walk around her, slowly circling her body, taking in every curve and contour of her exquisite form. I can feel the tension building within me, the desire to unleash myself upon her, to take her in a way that we've never experienced before.

I approach her from behind, gently brushing the crop's tip over the delicate skin at the backs of her thighs. She trembles slightly, her breathing becoming shallower with each passing moment. "Do you like this?" I ask, running the implement lightly over her back and shoulders, where her skin is bare above the red dress.

She gasps slightly at the sensation, her muscles tensing, her body responding to my every touch. "Yes," she murmurs, her voice barely audible over the thumping of the music outside the room.

I slowly bring the crop down against the backs of her bare thighs, starting lightly and gradually increasing the force. Each stroke is carefully calculated to create a wave of pleasure and pain that seems to consume every inch of her.

As I continue my teasing of her body, I can feel myself getting lost in the rhythm of the music and the crop and the tension between us. It's like we're in another world where time and space don't exist, where it's just us and the energy between us.

Freya's skin flushes from the crop.

"Do you want more?" I whisper into her ear, my voice barely above a murmur. "Do you want me to take you? Right here, right now, your wrists chained. With you being totally out of control?"

She shudders, her breath catching in her throat as she nods vigorously. The desire to be taken by me, to surrender completely to my control, is obvious in her every movement.

"Too bad." I can feel the adrenaline rushing through my veins, my heart pounding in time with the music. I want to take her, to plunge deep inside of her and claim her completely. I know she's not ready. "This is not the place or the time for me to take you for the first time, pretty Freya. But I will make you come. Hard and fast, till your knees go weak."

I kneel before her, reaching up under her dress, tugging her lacy elastic thong down over her hips, drawing them down till they're wrapped around her, mid-thigh. Her enchanting scent calls to me, and I can't resist an opportunity to put my mouth on her.

Licking and teasing, I get a taste of intoxicating Freya. "Oh. God." Her eyelids flutter.

I need to prepare her to ensure she's ready for what's to come. Forcing myself to unbury my mouth from her, I step back, picking up a small bottle of my preferred lubricant from the nearby table. I generously apply it to my fingers, slicking them up as I approach Freya again. She looks at me with fear, anticipation, and a burning desire that ignites a bonfire in my core.

"I'm going to touch you now," I whisper into her ear, "and I want you to let go of any fears or reservations. Just focus on the pleasure and sensations building within you."

I slowly run my slick fingers over her entrance, feeling the warmth and wetness that seems to emanate from her very core. Her body trembles slightly, her muscles clenching in anticipation of the promised release.

As I begin to insert one finger, then two, inside of her, Freya lets out a small gasp of pleasure. Her eyes roll back slightly as she loses herself in the moment, her body awash with a wave of pleasure. I continue to explore her inner depths, my fingers stroking and probing every inch of her sensitive flesh. Her breathing becomes heavier, her heart pounding faster as she surrenders entirely to my touch.

"Are you ready?" I ask, my voice a low rumble that seems to send her over the edge.

"I'm—I'm going to come." She shrieks, muscles locking around my fingers as she comes on my hand.

I remove my fingers, sliding them from her. She smiles at me. "That was incredible—"

"I'm not done, princess." She gives me a curious look. "Part your legs."

Obediently, she spreads her feet further apart till the restriction of the thong around her thighs stops her. I grab the crop, moving closer. She watches, wide-eyed in shock, as I bring the handle of the crop between her thighs.

I replace my fingers with the handle of the crop. It's cold and hard, contrasting with my warm fingers. She's so wet as I slowly insert it inside her, feeling the tightness of her muscles as they resist my invasion. But she wants this, needs this, and soon, she surrenders to my intrusion.

Then, I flick the button, turning on the vibrating handle.

She skyrockets onto her tiptoes, chains rattling as her back arches. "Oh my God!"

As I begin to thrust steadily, slowly but relentlessly, into Freya with the crop's vibrating handle, she lets out a soft moan of pleasure and pain. Her body shakes and trembles as she surrenders completely to the sensations that are building within her.

"That's it," I whisper, my voice hoarse with desire. "Let yourself go. Let me take you wherever this takes you."

I watch her beautiful face as I use my other hand to rub lube against her swollen clit. "Oh. My. God." Freya's breathing quickens, her body arching and twisting with every thrust of the crop, each circle from the pad of my thumb over her sensitive clitoris.

"Look at me," I command. "Look at me while I make you come."

Her eyes lock with mine, and I can see the depth of her desire mirrored in their depths. It's an intense and powerful exchange that only fuels the burning fire between us. I turn up the power on the vibrator.

"Holy. Fuck." She's no match for the intensity of what's inside her. As Freya's body begins to tremble uncontrollably, her orgasmic release washes over her in waves. "FRED. RICK."

"That's it," I whisper, moving my thumb faster, my voice thick with desire. "Let go, give in, let yourself fall completely into this moment."

"God! Fredrick! Fuuuuck!" she screams into the empty room, her arms stretching up, her body taut. "Fuck!"

Slipping the crop from inside her, I toss it to the floor. I kiss her lips, kissing her through the aftershock waves of the orgasm as she shudders against me. Still kissing her, I reach up, pressing a button on each cuff to unlatch them, freeing her wrists.

Her arms collapse and she wraps them around my neck, holding me tight as we kiss.

I feel so close to her now; I know she needed this escape. To my complete and heavenly shock, she drops to her knees. Gazing up at me with those sexy green eyes, she runs the tip of her tongue over her bottom lip, those pretty fingers with their sparkly silver tips going to my belt buckle.

"Nom de Dieu!" I reach up, gripping the chains in my hands for something to anchor me to this world as her perfect mouth wraps around my already pulsing cock. "God damn."

Soon, I'll have to break this spell by telling her about my earlier phone call with Callum. He called as we were leaving the house, heading for the club. The news he shared with me will surely break her heart.

Freya will probably never be safe in Glasgow.

And never be able to go back to her beloved home.

But this moment?

I'm holding on to those chains, letting her blow my mind.

Chapter Twelve

F reya

RETURNING TO NORSE GARDEN, I SLIP OFF MY heels and flop onto my bed like I've just come home from a long night at the club.

Did I say Norse Garden?

Gah!

I mean here at Wee Inverness.

The place must be growing on me.

What's even more dangerous?

The man is growing on me.

I wonder how long he'll be okay with our sexcapades being what they are? He's not a teen boy behind the bleachers. He's a man. One day, he's going to want real sex.

I'm not sure I'm there...

In school, I did things to look older and act older, and I wanted nothing more than for people to think I was older than I was.

But inside, I was still just a girl.

There was a teacher. One who was inappropriate with me, to put it delicately.

Now, it angers me.

Then, it just scared me.

He never did more than touch me under my bra, but the psychological damage was done.

I prayed for him to stop, but he didn't. I graduated, lost my religion, and left the island.

But I never lost my virginity.

I am still determining when I will. I've tried. Of course, I've tried. Have you seen how gorgeous they grow men in Glasgow? Och! Try as I might, I can't make myself cross that line.

Once a man is my husband, when I have a lifelong commitment from a man, I'll have the blessing of the island, and then I hope I'll be comfortable having intercourse.

That was my plan.

Then along comes Fredrick and his frisky tongue.

I might cross that line sooner than I thought. Last night at the club, if he had given in to me, I would have let him pop my wild Scottish cherry right there. But he knew it wasn't the right moment.

That's a man I respect. I mean, it would have been a hell of a way for a nearly thirty-year-old woman to lose it, but hey, how he wielded that riding crop—oh, mon Dieu!

I push the thought away, opting for a long soak in the tub to wash away the club. The dim light, the soft jazz music I'm playing in the background, the warm, sudsy water, the sound of the jet still pouring steaming water into the oversized soaker—it takes me back to that moment in the club, his hands on me, the look of control and dominance in his eyes.

My wrists cuffed to chains...

"Okay, mingey-boo, let's think of something else!" Instead of reawakening all that arousal, I finish my soak and dry off with a warm, plush towel—whoever invented towel warmers was pure dead brilliant—then slip into my jammies and take out my tablet. I'm not allowed to contact people, but a few untraceable sites have been approved, their connection directly linked to the house's Wi-Fi.

Tapping away with my long, pointy, silver-glitter fake nails, I pull up Christmas décor ideas. If I can't have Christmas at Norse Garden this year, I will decorate this wee castle.

I go to sleep, dreaming of two-story-tall Christmas trees filling his grand foyer, miles of fresh greenery lit with white and tied with red velvet, bringing the fragrance of fresh fir into the holiday-scented air.

I wake, ready to pounce on Fredrick, tell him what we'll collectively be working on today.

Dressed in emerald-green tights, a green-and-gold dress, and gold gift box replica earrings clipped to my lobes, I prance down the stairs in platform knee-high velvet boots, declaring, "It's Christmas!"

Fredrick is waiting for me at the bottom of the stairs. He wears a charcoal-gray V-neck sweater and black pants, and one arm rests on the wide, solid wood railing.

His thick dark hair is swept back, and a silver watch is on his wrist. I'm getting MAJOR hot dad vibes from him, and I love it.

He stares up at me, really leaning into the role with a stern daddy look on his handsome face. "It's December first," he corrects. "It's not Christmas yet."

"It's Christmas-TIME," I correct him back. "Just as worthy of being celebrated."

This brings a grin to his handsome face. He reaches up, cupping my face, his silver watch glinting under the lights. "Ma chérie, anything to see your beautiful smile."

"We can decorate?" My heart does a little flutter, skipping a beat. He wants to make me happy. I should be careful, or I might be putting on that wedding dress I just relocated to the guest room closet this morning.

He nods. "Go crazy."

"Careful, you have no idea how Christmas-crazy I can go."

"I've seen your Halloween. I'll survive."

I lean down, planting a big ol' smooch on him. Just as I kiss him, Morven stomps by, mumbling something under her breath about vixens and spells and seductresses.

I call to her to stop her. "Oh, Morven, wait! I have something for you." I hop down off the last stair, rushing over to her.

She stands in the center of the foyer, wearing her favorite blue apron and thick-framed glasses. Her hands are on her hips, and she gives me a suspicious glance. "Hmm…what would that be, Miss Freya?"

I slip the foiled blister pack from my pocket. "Allergy pills from the best allergist in Glasgow. I had them shipped here for you. They arrived late yesterday afternoon." I hand her the pill package.

She takes it from me, easing her glasses down her nose to read the back. "What would I need this for?"

"Just in case you ever get a soft spot for Happy Halloween. It's getting colder outside. I'm sure he would love to come in for the winter."

"I have a heater in the barn—"

"Hush, Fredrick." I can picture Happy now, curled up in a tartan cat bed snug by the Christmas tree, looking dapper in a red collar with a bow tie and a bell, festive against his black fur.

"Harrumph," Morven says, eyeing me, then eyeing the pills.

"I've heard they work wonders. Even with seasonal allergies."

She returns her hard gaze to me, although there's a hint of trust in her eyes. "I *have* been a wee bit worried about him in the cold. I'll give them a try." A sliver of victory brightens my smile. "But don't think for a moment you two will bring a dog into this house. Dogs are drawn to that river, and gah! The mud in the spring! I will not be cleaning up after muddy footprints." She shuffles off without a goodbye, but she pops a pill out of the foil and slips the rest into the pocket of her apron.

I clap my hands, staring up at Fredrick. "Does this mean we can bring him inside now?"

"Let's give her a few days to let the medication work." He leans down, planting a kiss on the top of my head. "The house hasn't felt right without him. Thank you."

"A few days—three—tops. That gives me time to get him everything he needs."

"He has food, a home, and care. What can he possibly need?"

"Collars. Bow ties. Beds for every room. Scratching posts. Fancy bowls with his name on them." I shrug. "You know. The basics."

He smiles. "I guess we have some shopping to do."

Online shopping is excellent, but there's nothing like seeing the decorations in person, holding the fabric between your fingers, and smelling the scent of the candles.

"Any chance you can get me into town without putting us in danger?" I ask.

A twinkle warms his gaze. "I have a better idea."

A few hours later, my personal Father Christmas, aka Fredrick, and I are on a private shopping spree at the Harrods in Inverness. Room after room of beautiful things, enchanting scents, and the most gorgeous store decorating I've seen. As a wee girl on the island decorating our mantle for Christmas by arranging dried Strawberry grass in vases with scraps of red ribbon and placing them next to plain white candlesticks, Harrods in December is me dying and going to holiday heaven.

And to have it all to our wee selves?

DEAD. Brilliant.

I politely ask Fredrick if they could crank up the Christmas music since it's just us. They do. Staff hit the perfect balance of bringing us cups of hot, spiced tea, bites of Christmas sweets and candies, and giving us privacy to enjoy the displays.

It's quite romantic. I peek at Fredrick as he examines a display of cashmere sweaters for both men and women. He's so damn handsome. And he's here with me, making my Christmas dreams come true.

My uterus throbs, wetness dampening my cotton Christmas tree panties. I toss my hair over my shoulder, demanding my minge to calm. "Whatcha looking at."

"Sweaters," he says. But he doesn't meet my eye. And his voice is low, pained, almost.

I put down the red silk hairband I was examining, giving him my full attention. I place a hand on his shoulder and ask, "Would you like one?"

He clears his throat. "It's silly."

"What? Tell me."

"I always wanted...matching."

"Matching sweaters?" This is NOT a conversation I ever thought I would have with this man.

He nods. "Like those magazines. With the families. The husband and wife. In the sweaters."

My heart almost bursts out of my chest. Fredrick Frisque, devoid of childhood love, wants to wear matching holiday sweaters with me?

"Let's do it!" I pick up the navy sweater with green-and-gold plaid stripes he's eyeing. "This one?"

He glances at the hairband I was holding a moment ago. "That won't match your hairband, though." He picks up a red, green, and white plaid sweater instead. "Would you like this better?"

"It is more festive." I pull the red bow tie bell cat collar from my bag. "And we will match with Happy."

He stares at me a long time before finally saying, "K." He pinches the bridge of his nose, composing himself. I look away, giving him a moment to himself.

Who'd have thought matching sweaters would bring a man to tears?

"Should we get silly sweaters for the staff as well?" I point to the ugly Christmas sweater section, which features Father Christmas squeezing his way down a chimney, a tackily decorated tree, and a gingerbread man who might be on acid.

"Yes, we should. I'd love to see Enrique don a reindeer sweater." He picks one of the red cashmeres in each of our sizes, cradling them in his arms. "But not this style. These are only for us."

I pluck up the red hairband, following him with the excitement of the puppy we're not allowed to have, to the tacky Christmas sweater table.

After shopping, we're invited to the Christmas tree-filled solarium, where I'm almost blinded by the bling hanging from their scented branches. We dine on tomato soup with fresh croutons and sandwiches. For dessert, he orders himself sparkling water; I'm spoiled with a spiked frozen hot chocolate.

It arrives with whipped cream. And sprinkles. "This is the most delicious thing I've ever tasted."

"I disagree." He reaches over to swipe whipped cream from the tip of my nose. He slides his finger between his lips, tasting. "You had something superior in your mouth last night."

I choke on a mouthful of cream and sprinkles. "Fredrick! We're at HARRODS, for goodness' sake. Even a wild islander like me knows you don't bring up," I whisper, *"blowjobs."*

We spend the rest of the day touring the small warehouse behind the store where commercial decorators can order. At first, the saleswoman looks at me like, "you need commercial décor?"

Then I pop off with, "I have an ENTIRE castle to decorate. And it is December One. I'm behind."

Hearing that, she's suddenly my best friend.

As we peruse the offerings of the warehouse, the saleswoman—"call me Missy"— flutters her lashes, trying to tempt attention from Fredrick, who she's rudely assumed OWNS Wee Inverness, saying, "And for you, Mr. Frisque? What style of Christmas do you enjoy?"

Luckily for Fredrick, he knows where his whipped cream is whisked, and he redirects his attention to me. "Madame will be choosing everything. Please, have your staff make sure it's to her liking."

Och! If he wasn't growing on me before tonight...

"Thanks, honey," I joke, slipping my arm around his waist, fluttering my own mascara-kissed lashes at Miss Missy.

Smooth as always, he slides an arm around my shoulders, kissing my cheek. "Of course, ma chérie. Anything to see you smile." The way he says it makes me feel that any woman fluttering her lashes at him would not get his attention.

My wee heart pitter-patters.

We finish our rounds and place our order. Fredrick pays. We go home. Well, back to his place to wait for the deliveries to begin.

We're settled in the cozy living room, a fire in the stone fireplace warming us, sharing a thin-crust pizza between us. My parcels from Harrods are stacked on the floor next to the coffee table. I thank him for the hundredth time that day.

I give a happy sigh. "That was the most fantastic day. I still can't believe you got us Harrods all to ourselves."

"Anything to bring a smile to your face, princess."

I blush under his attention. "Let's try on our sweaters," I say, pulling them from the tissue paper in their boxes.

He agrees. We laugh as we slip them over what we're already wearing, testing them out. I feel like I'm hanging out with my hawt best friend.

They're adorable. "Let's take a selfie—whoops! I don't have a phone, do I?"

"I bought you something to help with that. I know you miss your selfies." He walks over to the rolltop desk in the corner of the room, taking a small, silver-wrapped package out. He hands it to me. It feels heavier than it looks.

"What could this be..." In the package is a sleek digital camera. It looks high-tech, nothing like the cheap one I had as a teen. "Wow! Thank you so much."

Together, we take it out of the box and figure out how to work it. "Sit right there. You can be my first victim."

"Model?" he corrects.

"Same difference." I arrange him in a chair by the fire. The camera loves him. He's even more photogenic than I assumed he would be.

I glance down at the screen. "You look like the dad from those ads."

"Let me see." I walk over to him, showing him the screen. He pulls me down, so I'm sitting in his lap. "Take one of us."

I hold the camera out, facing the lens toward us. "Smile." I click the button. Together, we stare at the image of ourselves in matching sweaters; the couple in the photo is perfect, happy, and meant to be.

Staring at the photo makes me wish Callum and Fiona were also here to have me take their pictures. I've been so busy that I haven't processed the fact that I've been missing them. I don't mean to get quiet, but I do.

He surprises me by reading my mind. "Let's ask security if we could call Callum and Fiona."

"Can we do that?" I ask.

"Not often, but if we use the landline to call the landline at Norse Garden, we could probably pull one off safely. Let me chat with some people, and I'll be right back."

"Okay. I'll be here." I pop up from his lap so he can go. "In my sweater."

"Don't move," he says. I strike a silly pose, freezing in place. He chuckles, leaving me with a grin.

Nerves or excitement, I'm not sure which, flutter in my belly. It's been so long since we've spoken. Will the conversation be awkward? I nibble on the corner of a slice of pizza. A few minutes later, he returns with one of those large cordless battery-operated phones in his hand.

"A landline phone and a digital camera. I feel like I popped out of a time machine."

"All good. It'll work." He raises his brows. "Ready?"

My excitement turns to nerves. "I...think?"

He pulls me over to the sofa, sinking beside me. I watch as he presses the buttons on the phone, dialing a number I've never used, having no need to call the Norse Garden landline in the past.

"Am I doing this right?" he asks.

I peer over his shoulder. "I think you have to hit the button with the wee green phone on it after you dial."

"That should do it. Declan said Callum and Fiona will be waiting for our call." He pushes the speakerphone button. My heart is pounding by the second ring.

Fiona's bright, singsong-y voice comes over the phone, greeting me in Gaelic. "Halò!"

I mean, greeting us. I never felt like a third wheel with Callum and Fiona, but it's nice being a part of a couple. We're on a double date with two of my favorite people. "Heya, you two! How are you?" I look at Fredrick; he smiles at me, saying hello to them as well.

"Missing you like crazy!" Fiona giggles at her outburst. "It's so boring here without my wild Freya."

"God, yes," Callum says. "I'm missing yer bad renditions of 70s songs. It's so quiet here."

"Aww!" Relief floods me, nerves dissipating at the sound of their words. "We miss you, too. Fiona, you'll never believe what we did today. There is a Harrods. In Inverness! Och, and he has a CAT."

From there, the conversation turns to me and Fiona gabbing at breakneck speed. The blokes throw in a chuckle or murmur of agreement where appropriate. I want to ask Callum a million questions about Glasgow, the law firm, the islanders, and the Kings, but it's been so long since we've spoken that I choose to keep things light instead.

The topic turns to Christmas Day. Callum interjects. "Fredrick and I have spoken, Freya. We can make safe plans to join you in Inverness for Christmas. Would you like that?"

I stare at Fredrick in shock. I didn't even think a visit would be possible. I've been decorating this place, thinking it would just be him and me. And Happy. "Are ye joking? That would be dead brilliant."

"Can you handle feeding us with your staff off for the holiday, Freya?" Fiona teases.

"We'll manage," Fredrick says.

"Somehow," I add. "Fiona, am I allowed to use the microwave?"

"Lord, no!" she laughs. "Cheffie still complains about the burnt popcorn smell."

Fredrick gets brave, saying, "We'll cook."

"I'll research a good number for a local pizza place in Inverness that is open for Christmas." Callum laughs. "Under caution."

"Please! Have ye so little faith? We've got this, don't we, Fredrick?"

"Absolutely." He lifts a fist for a bump. I tap it. We all talk for another hour, joking, laughing, and keeping things light. When I see them in person, I figure that'll be the appropriate time to ask for updates.

I will also be able to ask Callum when his plans for my arranged marriage first began.

As they leave the call, my heart shatters in my chest. Of course, it will be lovely to have them visit. But everything will always be different between us now, won't it?

We're no longer the three musketeers. Now, it's Callum and Fiona. And me and Fredrick. But for how long will it be Fredrick and me? How long will he let me stay here without giving in to his marriage demands?

The decisions we make, knowingly or unknowingly, shape our futures.

I ignored Callum's fears, worries, and warnings. While partying isn't wrong, I could have appeased him, encapsulating myself better in the Kings' protection, so I wasn't an easy target for the Hoax. And to reassure my brother, who only had my well-being at heart, I could have taken the car when he asked, kept my phone on me, and stayed on the grid.

If I'd been more careful, maybe I wouldn't have made the mistake that changed everything.

I crossed that line.

And there's no going back.

Chapter Thirteen

Freya

I don't want him to see me cry. We've gotten so close so quickly; he has done everything to make me feel welcome, special, and beautiful. I don't want to make him think I'm running away from him.

"I'm getting hot in all these layers. I need to—change. I'll be right back."

Knowing there's something wrong, he follows me up the stairs. Silent. I enter my bedroom, holding the door open to him as an invitation. I flop down on the bed. He sits beside me where I lie.

Not wanting to talk about my pain, I grab his hand. "Tell me about your mother," I say. "If that's okay..."

He looks down at me. "I'd love to share with you. It's a heavy story, though. Should we save it for another night?"

"Tell me." He lies beside me, and I curl up on his chest, ready to listen.

"She suffered from depression. My father was not an easy man to live with. I don't know which came first, my father or the low mood, but either way, she struggled. She built this garden in the back of our home. Her calming garden, she called it. It was meant to be beautiful, but I always found it eerie with the vines creeping up the stone walls. There was a big tree, a massive oak." His voice catches, and he takes a moment.

I reach up, touching his face. "You don't have to continue. I shouldn't have asked."

"No, I want to share this with you." He takes a shaky breath. "One day, this world was all too much for her. I couldn't find her anywhere. The last place I looked was her garden. There she was...hanging from the tree."

"Oh my God!" I gasp, covering my mouth with my hands, sorry for my outburst. I quiet myself, wanting to be calm for him. "You saw your mother...and you were a child."

"Only ten..." His voice trails off.

We're silent for a moment, him thinking of his mother, me thinking of how strong he is, how this would have shaped him. Glancing up at his face, I see the pain. All I want in this moment is to take that pain away.

There are no words to ease his pain. So, I kiss him. A deep kiss filled with wanting. A kiss to let him know how much I love being here with him and how much I trust him, as much as he trusts me.

Slowly, we take one another's clothing off. We lie back down on the bed, kissing. My mind strays, thinking of how much

I've grown to trust this man, how I trust him implicitly with my body.

The first time he tried to touch my breast, I freaked.

We were in the Great Hall, and he was sucking, nipping, as he is now, surely leaving marks on my skin as he did at that moment. He smoothed a hand down my side, over my stomach, brushing over my breast—

And the awful, icky feeling filled me, instantly robbing me of all the heady, sensual ones that had me on cloud nine only a moment ago. I tore his hand away, saying no.

The heat of humiliation washed over my shame-filled face. And he...

He said, "I understand." He told me to tell him if he ever does anything that doesn't feel good to me. Then, he made me feel amazing; my body responded to his every touch and kiss. Like he's doing now, exploring every inch of my body while being so careful to avoid my breasts.

I categorized him, putting us in neat little boxes that night, letting our sexcapades escalate while our relationships remained stagnant, deadlocked in the place of the tug and pull we'd been caught in. Now, as we lie together, naked, bared, the warmth of our bodies pressing together, I feel closer to him than I've felt to anyone.

He stops kissing me to look at me, brushing my hair away from my face. He holds my gaze. "You're so beautiful."

"So are you." In this moment, our eyes lock. I take his hand in mine, bringing it to my breast. I cup his palm over my breast, feeling his warmth, fighting through the ick till it's just him and only his hand on me.

His eyes widen. "Are you sure?" he asks.

I nod. Holding him there, I kiss him.

A warm shiver runs down my spine as his lips move to gently graze my delicate skin. The sensation of his mouth on my breast is unlike anything I have experienced before, and it only intensifies the desire that slowly consumes me. His hands, firm and gentle at the same time, cup my breast as he continues to kiss and nibble my tight nipple.

My breath quickens as he gently pinches my other nipple, feeling it harden beneath his touch. A soft moan escapes me, eliciting a smile from him as he continues. Staring down at his face, his closed eyes, his expert mouth smiling around my breast as he worships it for the first time…the way he looks is so sensual I almost come.

He reaches up to brush a stray hair out of my face. "You are so beautiful," he murmurs. "I've never felt so connected to someone before."

I smile back at him. "Me too. I want…" Unable to say the words, I stare into his eyes. He reads me. He moves closer to me, his lips hovering just above mine. His breath is hot against my skin as he speaks again. "Are you sure you're ready for this? We can wait if you want."

I take a deep breath and nod, feeling a surge of bravery. "I want this. I want you. I trust you."

"Such a gift." He leans in and kisses me gently, his lips soft and sweet against mine. I feel myself relax into the kiss, letting go of all my inhibitions. His hands roam over my body, leaving trails of fire in their wake. I arch into his touch, wanting more and more of him.

His lips travel down my neck, and tingles travel to my core. I close my eyes and let myself get lost in the feeling of him. This is the man, the moment I've been waiting for. What my body has been craving.

His touch is slow and deliberate, each caress sending shivers down my spine. But as his fingers dip into me, I can't help but wonder if I'm ready for this. His knee nudges at my inner thigh, spreading me open, and I feel vulnerable and exposed.

Our eyes are locked in a heated gaze as he hovers over me. As he finally enters me, I let out a sharp gasp, feeling the pain and pleasure collide. He continues to watch me intensely, but I can see the concern etched on his face.

"Are you okay, Freya?" In this moment, I'm not sure if I can handle this, but I don't want to disappoint him either. Brushing my hair back from my face, he asks again, "Are you okay?"

I struggle to find the words to answer. "Yes," I manage to say, unsure if it's the truth or just what I want him to hear.

As his hands move across my body, I feel conflicted. On the one hand, the stress and worries of the outside world seem to fade away, leaving only a burning desire for him. But at the same time, I can't help but feel a tightness in my chest, knowing that this moment is fleeting and will eventually end.

Will I still trust him like this in the morning?

Will he still want me?

As he enters, a tidal wave of physical and emotional tension crashes over me. My body wants to welcome him fully, but my mind is holding back in fear—my anxiety is not allowing me to let go completely.

He senses my turmoil and brushes his lips against my forehead, cheeks, and chin. "Ma chérie, my princess," he whispers, his voice soothing and reassuring. "I'll never hurt you. Let me make you feel good."

My heart races at his words, and I take a deep breath to calm myself. As I release it, he thrusts completely into me with force and speed, filling me. My breath catches in my throat as he stretches me beyond what I thought was possible. He's so big, and the pleasure combined with a hint of pain leaves me gasping for air. But I trust him and know he will take care of me in this moment.

He starts to move faster inside me now, every thrust sending heat through my body. My skin is on fire, and my heart is racing with the moment. I reach up to meet his lips, our tongues twisting. The intensity builds, each movement more powerful than the last. He grips me tightly, our skin slick with sweat, our bodies moving in perfect unison.

"Yes," I murmur against his lips, my voice hoarse with desire. "Harder."

He takes me up on my challenge, thrusting deeper into me, his hips slamming against me. I cry out in delight and pain.

Our hearts beat wildly together, our breaths ragged and uneven.

"I need you," he growls, his voice rough with need. "I need you now." He flips us over, me now sitting on top of him—another new, overwhelming sensation.

I take a moment to orient myself with my hands on his chest. My hair curtains the sides of my face as I look down at him. I move my hips, trying to get used to the new, strange, intoxicating sensation of his hardness inside me.

His voice is a rake over hot coals. "Dance for me, Freya."

His sexy words release my remaining inhibitions. I let go, throwing my head back, running my hand through my hair, arching my back, and riding.

He holds me tightly, his hands gripping my hips as he guides my movements. Our breaths quicken. His desire is evident in the way his body moves beneath mine, every thrust hungry for me.

"I'm going to make you come," I say, riding him hard.

"God, you're so fucking sexy."

Every muscle in my body tenses as I cling to him, feeling the heat radiating from his skin and the strength in his arms. The room is filled with an intoxicating mixture of our combined sweat and passion.

Our eyes lock, and we share a brief moment amidst the chaos. Everything else fades away for a split second, leaving only the two of us caught up in this. About to come, I feel a sudden need to be closer to him.

I lean over, and he rises to meet me, our lips tangling in a passionate kiss, his hands in my hair, our bodies curling around one another, a tight knot of tension.

Then, we find our release.

"God! Fredrick!" I clamp down tight, burying him inside me, chasing down that final rasp of friction my body so desperately craves. I feel the orgasm throughout my entire body this time. Warmth, energy, liquid release. He comes inside me, heat and wetness, so full it runs out of me, wet and hot between my thighs. I collapse against him, catching my breath.

He holds me there, just like that.

Afterward, we shower, change into pajamas, and move to his bed for the night. The first night we've spent in the same room. I'm sure we won't go back to separate rooms after this.

Finally, I ask the question burning in my mind since he shared with me the story of his mother. "How do you live with the pain?"

Fredrick smooths my hair, thinking. "I face my past, my pain, directly. I don't hide it, don't push it away. If that image... of my mother comes to mind, I watch it pass by like a scene from a film. I allow myself to experience the emotions. Then, I let it go. Knowing it will be back."

"Hmm." I process his words, wondering if I could do as he does.

"Ma chérie, you push the difficult times away. As you know, the pain will return. When you don't embrace the emotions, you give them strength. Each time they return, they come back stronger. And if you don't face them head-on, one day it may all come rushing back so strong, it swallows you whole." He strokes my cheek. "'*On ne voit clairement qu'avec le cœur.*' We only see clearly with the heart."

"That's pretty." I mull over his words. "Is that a French saying?"

"From the book, *The Little Prince*." His voice lowers. "My mother used to read it to me."

Beautiful.

Fredrick's right. I push things down. Now, I stare at my life point-blank.

"I want to tell you about Jack. The case that ended up bringing me here."

He lifts my hand to his lips, kissing each finger in turn. "Please. Share."

"I was riding high off a win I'd just had against Patrick, when Jack first approached me about representing him," I tell Fredrick.

"What was your meeting with Jack like?"

I flush under his attention; he always seems interested in my life, my thoughts, my idiot-syn-crazies. I tell him, "I invited Jack into my office. He sat in the chair across from me at my desk. He beamed a stunning grin, and I got caught in the beam."

"As I'm sure he was caught in a cloud of your beauty." He sends me a flirty quirk of a brow. "I can picture you at your desk. Black suit? Ten-meter heels?"

"Always." I give a choked laugh, shaking my head at his compliments. "In my self-importance, I wanted to prove to him that I could win his case. I was more focused on celebrating, partying, and whisky than on vetting him. Knowing his dad, I didn't investigate Jack as I should have."

The case came so fast; the firm was already dead busy, and no one checked behind me—they didn't think they had to.

A tear slips down my cheek. Fredrick kisses it away. I wrap my arms around his neck.

He clears his throat. "I made a similar mistake when I first brought you here. I was drawn to your strength, then ignored what made me want you. I thought I could force you into a wedding gown…and that would make you mine."

Reaching over me to flip open the lid of a wooden box on the nightstand, he says, "Now I know you can't take what can only be given freely."

Staring into my eyes, he holds up a ring I may have designed for myself—a simple yet generously sized, brilliant, emerald-cut diamond with a high setting on a thick platinum band. The light hits the diamond, casting rainbows.

"It's stunning." I absorb the ring, taking in its brilliance and everything it stands for. We may not be in love, but we've become best friends with delicious benefits. I know he'll take care of me, protect me—and continue giving me phenomenal orgasms.

Most of all, with Fredrick, I'm getting the security I crave.

"You belong here. You belong with me." He slips the ring on my finger.

And in the contentment of my afterglow, I let him.

Chapter Fourteen

F redrick

WHEN I FIRST BOUGHT THIS PLACE, THE GARDEN was stripped and barren. I promised myself I'd do something with it in my mother's memory. I haven't even been past the garden gates.

It was traumatizing to be the one who found her hanging from the tree in the garden. After that day, I was sent off to boarding school. My mother's name never left my father's mouth again.

Was there therapy back then? Child psychologists? I'm not that old, but I assume such things were around.

But not available to a young boy who stood under his mother as her body swayed, her blank eyes staring up accusingly toward the massive, cold home she could no longer live in.

How I wanted those eyes to look down at me.

To give me that wink she did when my father was going on about something, some rant about the price of shipping, to tell me how silly all this was, the house, the money, the name.

She didn't fit into our lives. And she couldn't force herself to not laugh too loud at the stuffy parties, always having one drink too many.

So, my father took away the alcohol till she had nothing left to rely on. And now, I spend my life brewing the amber liquor that comforted her. And, knowing how it got ahold of her, I rarely drink other than the tastings required to confirm what I already know.

It's the best in Scotland.

My father trapped her in the stone walls of our French estate, and she threw herself into gardening.

Her calming garden.

But the plants and flowers weren't enough to get her through.

When your family has money and a name to uphold, your troubled mother suddenly has an undiagnosed, underlying heart defect and dies in her sleep.

And as for you?

Apparently, you've shown "great talent" in the languages and now, out from under your mother's wing, want to commit your (ten-year-old) self to education.

Fucked up?

Yes. Even at ten, I knew this was not a healthy family dynamic, though I knew nothing different.

Marriage, a wife, and children to carry on our name we so brutally kept clean; I want it all. Like I told her at Harrods, I want the smiling family in the magazine ads.

Thus, an arranged marriage to a beautiful, brilliant, strong woman who happens to love the taste of my whiskey, one who will make the perfect mafia wife and adoring mother, suits me perfectly.

Attachment, love…I'm afraid my capacity for those frivolous things died on that tree.

I think Freya's aware of that fact.

I was stunned when she kept the ring on her finger.

I've never been a giddy little kid on Christmas morning, but I think the way I feel right now, staring at the ring on her perfect finger as we lounge here in bed, has to come close to the feeling of seeing that Father Christmas loaded with your tree with gifts.

Ma chérie, my fiancée.

The most precious gift she's given me for Christmas was letting me touch her in a place where she is most vulnerable. I've never had someone trust me that deeply with their body. It was an intense moment, and I knew it was the perfect time to give her the ring.

I had it made months ago.

Now, lying here, our breathing slowing, her wearing the ring I've envisioned on her so many times, I feel as if it's the right time to ask her about her past pain. I grab her hand, intertwining our fingers as we stare at the ring.

"It's beautiful," she says. "Thank you."

"It looks like you." We lie quietly, and finally, I say, "You don't have to tell me. But what happened?"

"There was a teacher at our school on the island," she starts. "The only male teacher we'd ever had. He was handsome. I had a schoolgirl crush, and in the way a fourteen-year-old girl does, I flirted with him. After class, I hung around his desk, rolling up my skirt and wearing lipstick. Just innocent stuff to get his attention."

She stops a moment and gives a hard swallow. I place my hand over hers, feeling her warmth and the coolness of the new ring. "You don't have to finish."

"I want to." She brushes a tear away. "You shared with me, and I'd like to share with you."

"Thank you." I lift her hand to my lips, kissing it once before setting it back down.

She takes a shuddering breath and gives me a tight smile in her bravery. "Anyway, one day, he started to react to my attention. First," she looks away, "he would just reach down during class, discreetly snapping my bra strap through my shirt." A flush rises in her cheeks. "Sometimes...the other girls saw. They turned on me, calling me—ugly names. It was horrible. Humiliating."

I want to kill him. And if I ever cross paths with this man, I will. "I'm so, so sorry."

She keeps going: "Then...things progressed. He had me stay after school. He told me to come sit on his lap. But nothing sexual." She shakes her head, shiny hair gliding over her shoulders. "Just sitting.

"A few weeks later, he started to slide his hand down the front of my shirt, cupping my breast. He said...he said he liked—ugh, this is so gross..."

"You don't have to say it."

"It's okay. I've never told anyone. It's just hard. But it's a relief too." She gazes up, looking for strength. "He said he liked the feel of mine because they were so small, still growing."

My stomach turns. I want to throw up and commit murder all at once. How dare he do that to her? And how many others has he gone on to abuse?

I swallow down my anger, focusing on her. "Did he do anything else? Touch you anywhere else?"

She gives a choked laugh. "That's as far as it went. Still, I knew things had already gone too far. I didn't know how to go back. I felt icky, yucky, ashamed. I thought if the women of the island were to find out, they'd blame me. The lipstick, the short skirt..." She sniffs. "Now, I know better. They would have driven him off the island with pitchforks."

"Were you able to tell anyone? Callum?"

"Gah, no! I was terrified to tell my brother. I knew he'd do something crazy. I didn't want him ending up in prison."

"Have you carried this weight with you, alone, all these years?"

"Yeah. And the worst part? I thought it would be over when I moved off the island, but it never was. Every boyfriend I had..." Her voice trails off. Suddenly, her eyes shoot up, locking on mine. "You are the first, the only, man who understood." With that, she throws her arms around my neck, melting against me. "Thank you."

Our naked bodies press together as I hold her tight. "I'll never, ever let anything happen to you. Ever."

If another man were even to make her slightly uncomfortable in his presence...

We sleep in one another's arms. In the morning, dressed in festive clothing, with our arms wrapped around one another's waists, we stare up at our perfect tree. I hear a bell tinkling and, following the sound, I glance over to find Joyeux running into the room, looking dapper in his red bow tie. He brushes against my ankles.

I scoop him up; he wiggles toward Freya, his new love. Unable to blame him for falling under her spell, I hand him over. She takes him, cooing at the cat. "Aren't you just a handsome little man? Have you seen our tree?" Looking back at the tree, she leans her head on my shoulder. "We make a good team. Don't we?"

"We do."

Overhearing as she walks by, MAWR-vein pats Joyeux, her allergies no longer an issue. "You certainly do make a pair," she says, surprising us both when she adds, "You've found your better half, sir. Don't let this one get away."

Freya beams at Morven's approval.

It's a perfect moment.

The thought brings back my fears that I'm not capable of giving her everything she needs.

The thing she needs most.

I don't know how to love someone. It's been so long, and even then, there was only one person. She was ripped away from me. I don't know if I can risk opening myself up again.

If I can love her the way she deserves.

I'll not deprive precious Freya of anything. If I am not capable of giving her everything she needs...

I will do the right thing.

Which is always the thing that seems impossible.

I will let her go.

Chapter Fifteen

F reya

NO WORK AND ALL PLAY MAKE FREYA A CRANKY mob wife. 'Scuse me. Fiancée.

I'm still getting used to the title. The ring already feels like an extension of me. Not only did he pick a gorgeous, flawless, brilliant diamond, but the piece is just—me.

He chose a ring so perfect that if I had my phone, I'd change his contact from *Freaky Freddie* to *Frisky Fiancé*. But I don't have a cell phone, and I'm still confused, and I've heard nothing from Callum.

Hence, there are no current plans for a wedding. Wearing the ring has been enough to appease him. With my whole world changing, I'm leery of making a lifelong commitment.

An engagement can be broken.

A marriage cannot. When I say vows, I mean them. I wish the Kings would realize that.

The girls at the firm have been told I'm back on the island, visiting my dear Aunt Mary. That she recently had a health issue, that she begged for me specifically, and that, in my selflessness, I've gone to stay with her and nurse her back to health.

It's a laugh.

The last time something was in my care, I was tasked with watering our neighbor's plants while she was on a month-long Alaskan cruise; I partied, forgot to water them, and they all died.

All the Kings in Glasgow and everyone on the island have been told I'm underground, hiding from the Hoax somewhere in the English countryside till we get this sorted out.

Sorted out meaning…what?

I don't yet know.

Maybe my people will finally come to their senses and remember who I am. From the outside looking in, it is a wee bit suspicious, especially how I carried on, partying to celebrate my win in court. How will I convince everyone I'm innocent while untangling myself from the Hoax's name?

Callum says I can't, and my job is to lay low, stay safe, and do as I'm told.

A feat I fear is too great for me to accomplish.

I'm out of my element now, relying on two men instead of myself. Fredrick to provide for me and protect me here in Inverness. Callum to sort out my life with the Kings. Christmas Day, over wine and pudding, Callum tried his best to avoid the subject, the conversation ending with him saying these things take time, that I'm impatient, and for ONCE, can he be the one in charge, and can I shut my wee mouth?

Wee mouth? HA! I could fit a whole haggis between these MAC Frost Pink lips.

Since my haggis-sized mouth gets me in trouble, I stay busy. With Christmas come gone and packed away, I turn to other projects. Wee Inverness is a beautiful blank slate with clean lines and good bones. It's a grand castle perched over a gorgeous river and quaint town, deserving of being her best, so I dive into renovations and let Callum sort out my life.

I'm installing an infinity pool, a rock waterfall wall dipping into a round in-ground hot tub, and a koi pond.

Also, I'm working on a surprise for Fredrick's garden. With a wee sneaky bit of help from Morven and her eccentric, reclusive artist husband, I've commissioned a piece for the garden's center. I want him to be able to visit anytime.

Fredrick is actively trying to keep me busy as well. It takes a lot of work. Especially when it's a holiday and he knows I'm missing the family, like today, New Year's Day. We rang in the new year with champagne and sexy times at midnight. It was fantastic; I'm still glowing.

Now, as we have been doing every morning since I officially took up residence in his—our—lovely owners' suite, we sit and have breakfast. We prefer the round table with the two chairs in the small living room off the main bedroom. Together, we sip coffee and nibble breakfast as we discuss our day.

Taking a sip of black coffee, he flips open his laptop, asking me ever so casually, "What would you like to do today?" as if it was just a typical day, with two average newlyweds—yikes, engaged people—ready to spend the day together.

We do make a striking couple.

Now, with more money than God, no need to work, and nothing but time on my perfectly manicured, diamond ring-covered fingers...what would I like to do today?

"Hmm..." I flutter my lashes. "I want to put on a black dress, high heels, a generous spray of Gucci Floral, and march into a courtroom to kick some ass."

"In time, ma chérie." His voice dips, his gaze lowering. "Have you considered another career in case it proves too dangerous for you to be back in the courts?"

His words hit me hard. "Seriously? Are things in Glasgow looking that bad for me?"

"I worry for you. I'm thinking maybe keep an open mind." He offers a soft smile. "That's all."

I sit there, stunned. I am a fierce female solicitor. It's my identity, my drive, my passion, my life. Have I thought of what I would do if I can't go back?

Walking the halls of Wee Inverness, Happy prancing at my side, his wee bell tinkling, this place is becoming more and more like my new home...I may have toyed with the idea of installing a fantastic west-wing spa and an east-bridal suite.

The estate would be a breathtaking place for weddings.

The wee thought may have slipped into my mind.

"Currently, I have no plans to change careers." I stab a berry with the prongs of my fork, popping it into my mouth. "We shall see."

"*Vivre l'instant present.* Let us focus on the present moment." He gives me an easy grin. "There must be something touristy you'd like to do today?" His eyes brighten. "Maybe a historical site with a detailed tour?"

I cast back my mind back, scanning childhood dreams of where we would travel when we finally left our isolated yet beautiful island. Wanting him to enjoy our day, too, I need a suggestion to quench his love of history. "Edinburgh Castle," I say. "I've never been there. Have you?"

"I've not." His dark eyebrows shoot sky-high. "But you? You're Scottish."

"Aye! Born and bred." I hold my Tunnocks teacake up in the air with pride. "Long live Scotland."

"How have you not been to Edinburgh?" he asks. He pours me a tassie of tea with a skoosh of milk, passing it to me.

"Thank you." I take a deep sip of the delicious tea, confirming he's gotten the ratio perfect.

"Do islanders not travel?" he asks.

"We're not the only ones." Peeling back the silver-and-red wrapper of my teacake, I inform him, "You'd be surprised how infrequently we in the United Kingdom do 'tourist things' even though they are right under our noses. I have a friend at the firm." A pang for my old life hits. "She was from a small town in England, living only an hour's train ride from London, and had never been. One of the most important cities in the world." I shake my head, stunned. "Can you imagine?"

"I cannot." He goes pensive. "The French explore and appreciate every inch of their beautiful country, from the cities to the Riviera to the peaceful countryside."

"Of course they do, because you all have a different wine and cheese to try at every stop." I eye him. "France is so beautiful. There is so much culture. And my goodness, I loved the food. Do you miss it?"

He casts his gaze over his hands. "Too many memories."

"Understood." I keep it light. "I adore Scotland, but France beats us in the delicacy department. We have haggis and sausage. There's only so much ground meat product one can partake of."

His nose wrinkles as if he's smelling the stuff. "What's haggis?"

"Did we not have it at the pub on St. Andy's Day?" I try to remember. Only chains and riding crops are coming to mind.

"I can't say that we did." A mischievous smile. He's thinking of the same memory.

"I guess we were doing things other than eating sheep entrails—never mind. You don't want to know what haggis is made of. Trust me."

"I'll take your word for it. And I think Edinburgh will make for a perfect day trip."

I'm always so impressed with how quickly he can type. His fingers fly over the keyboard as he searches.

I am the one at Norse Garden who always steers the ship and makes the plans. I must say it's nice to have someone besides me and Jesus take the wheel for once. With his elite upbringing, extensive travel experience, and excellent taste, Fredrick's almost as good a planner as me.

Och. Confession—even better than me. Le sigh.

Letting him do his thing, I flip through the newspaper he brings to the room every morning for our morning routine. I'm beginning to enjoy the feel of the paper between my fingers, missing my news app on my phone less and less. I sip at my soy latte sprinkled with cinnamon while nibbling at the warm chocolate croissant he ordered.

It's funny how quickly we've grown comfortable in our routine, how he's come to know all my likes and, more importantly, dislikes—veggie quiche, I'm looking at you, spinach and onions have no place at breakfast.

Fifteen minutes later, he snaps his laptop shut. Putting my paper down, I give him my full attention. "Lay it on me, tour guide. What are we getting up to on this lovely New Year's Day?"

"I'm so glad you asked." His brown eyes sparkle. What I used to confuse with cockiness I now know is a mischievous warmth. "First, we'll drive to Edinburgh."

"Complete with our entourage, I'm sure."

"Absolutely."

"Can we spare a wee bit of security today? Pretty please? Everyone will be so hungover from New Year's Eve that looking for us will be the furthest thing from their Hoaxy minds." I gasp a breath after my monologue, trying to describe the wave of emotion that comes over me on this sunny winter day. "I want to feel…"

He fills in my thoughts. "Normal?"

"Aye. Thank you." We've also been known to complete one another's sentences, which makes Morven's eyes roll to the back of her head. "I'd like to feel normal for a day."

"Thankfully, there is nothing normal about you, Freya Burnes." He waits a beat before saying, "But I'll see what I can do."

He loves to please me, and I try to reciprocate. I hope he sees that when I finish the garden.

Not wanting to be a problem, I say, "Whatever you think is best, of course, but I would love a casual day in the crowd, which is difficult, surrounded by burly circus men."

"We've been over this. Alex is not, nor has he ever been, a member of Fossett's Circus. Though I must admit that mustache is from another place and time." He leaves no space for me to chime in. "Moving on. I've blocked the day off into four, three-hour events."

"Of course you have," I tease, though I'm starting to fall for his direct, organized ways. I realize he's not stuffy; he knows what he likes and is confident about his choices.

"Three-hour drive, followed by a three-hour tour and visit at the castle, then a three-hour shopping spree—"

I hold up a finger, making an important point. "Where we will be purchasing wool sweaters to add to our collection."

"Absolutely." He nods. "It's kind of our thing."

"We *are* up to three sets. Harrods, the ones Morven brought us back from her trip, and those flashy green-and-pink golf ones we ordered after too much champagne last night."

"Three sets are not nearly enough." He shakes his head.

"After we shop, we'll dine at a local pub. No haggis, I promise. Then, three hours home."

"Just in time for our nightly cuddles with Happy."

"Yes, he's dying to know the ending of *Air Force One*." He grins.

I smile back, imagining our peaceful evening routine after such a busy day: the two of us cuddled on the couch in our similarly styled couture pajamas, Happy curled up in his favorite resting spot on the top of the sofa cushion behind the back of Fredrick's head as we watch movies.

Never having been allowed to waste time as a kid, Fredrick missed all the best American films, and I've taken it upon myself to catch him up.

Right now, we're on a Harrison Ford kick.

Returning to our day, I ask, "What does our time in the castle consist of?"

"I'm glad you asked!" He flips his laptop open, reading aloud. "'Embark on a guided tour. Go behind the scenes of the castle with a knowledgeable guide. Many claim this is an excellent way to spend a day—Marvel at the Crown jewels. Admire the oldest set of Crown jewels in the British Isles, first used together in 1543. Visit St Margaret's Chapel. Step inside Edinburgh's most ancient building, constructed around 1130 by King David I. See Mons Meg—'"

"Mons Meg?" Sounds suspiciously like something minge-y.

He nods. "Mons Meg. It says here: 'Look down the barrel of this massive siege gun capable of firing a 150kg gunstone up to two miles away.'"

"A cannon?"

"Not sure. But then we explore vaults, journeying into the areas that once held notorious pirate captives." He stops, eyes lingering on my body in the thin white robe I wear. "I could think of a naughty thing or two to do to you in those vaults."

"Och, stop." I flush, waving him away with my hand. "Please. Back to business."

"'Witness the One o'clock Gun. Watch as the One o'clock Gun is fired each day'—so it must be a cannon," he holds up a finger, "'excluding Sundays, Good Friday, and Christmas Day.'"

"Whew." I flip my hair. "Not our holiday, good. Open on New Year's Day. Continue."

"'Take in the stunning views,'" he reads. "'Soak in the breathtaking panoramic views of Edinburgh from atop Castle Rock.'"

"Och, selfie time!"

He groans inwardly, but I know he loves the pictures I snap of us on my digital camera. "Then we'll grab a bite to eat in the Tea Room located at the highest point of the castle."

"Love that!" A tea room means chocolate and pastries. My mouth is watering.

Reading my mind, he says, "I'll be finding you some source of protein as well."

"Spoilsport," I joke, loving the TLC.

"You'll need sustenance other than flour, sugar, and butter because we will climb the Lang Stairs. Here it says: 'Count all 70 steps on these original entrance stairs to the castle, then pass through Portcullis Gate: Walk under the menacing spikes of this fortified gateway, built nearly 450 years ago.'"

"Och! My calves are already feeling the burn."

He raises one brow. "I'll massage them tonight."

"I'm sure you'll try," I tease. "And I'm sure the tour guide will provide us titillating dates and historical facts to get your blood flowing."

"And I'm sure the sights will provide lovely backdrops for the million photos you demand of us, and the Tea Room will give you the daily sugar rush you require."

"To get up the seventy stairs."

"Protein builds muscle, which—never mind." He closes the laptop with finality, standing and stretching. "Shall we get ready for our day?"

"Let's." I join him, stretching up to wrap my arms around his neck for a kiss.

The kiss leads to tongue. I pull back to ask, "Tell me. What would you do if you had me all to yourself in one of those pirate vaults?"

"Mmm...all kinds of things, but what I want to do now is see what you're hiding under that flimsy robe, then bend you over this table and have my way with you." He smooths his hands over my ass, cupping my curves.

His touch sends a shiver down my spine. With a playful tone, I tease, "As tempting as that sounds, we should probably save that for another time. We have a castle to conquer first."

Chuckling, he reluctantly releases me, and we set about getting ready for our day of adventure.

As I brush my hair until it gleams down my back, I can't help but feel that we make the perfect pair.

Our meeting in the foyer punctuates my thoughts. We look at one another and laugh. We've unknowingly coordinated our travel wear, both in blue and white. I wear modest pearl earrings; my money piece is a breathtaking pearl necklace made of three strands, each a wee bit longer than the first, so they layer beautifully. I've paired it with a navy high-neckline fluttery skirted dress and no tights despite the cold—I will always sacrifice for fashion—with a cream-colored calf-length down coat, gloves, and scarf to fight the chill.

He wears a navy-and-white striped sweater, a white-collared shirt underneath, and a long, navy wool coat.

"You look very French. I love it." Easing over to him, I lock arms, taking us in. Secretly, I love the way we look together. I lie in bed at night, smiling about our matching sweaters. That is why I make him take so many photos with me. "Great minds think alike. We match."

He raises a brow. "You're going to take too many pictures of us today, aren't you?"

"Aye, you betcha!" I pat the matching cream leather bag at my side. "I've got my camera tucked away right here, love."

We settle into the warm back seat of the sleek black Bentley limousine, carefully folding and storing our outerwear for our arrival. As we drive toward Edinburgh, the anticipation builds within me. I can't help but feel grateful for having him by my side, guiding me through this new, unsure chapter of my life.

Sneaking a peek at him next to me on the black leather back seat of the car, I take in his profile—is it possible the man is even more handsome from this angle? That thick head of hair most men would kill for. The jaw locked in thought as he gazes out his window.

I run my hand up the back of his head, fingers sliding through his silk-like hair. "Your kids would have fantastic hair," I say.

"So would yours," he says.

I think about what our children would look like. Would they have his dark eyes and my contrasting light hair? A baby black pearl. Or a wee, curly-haired, green-eyed brunette?

A thought crosses my mind. I'm engaged to the man—no wedding plans in sight, still—and I don't even know. "Do you want children?"

"Absolutely. I want the wife, the marriage, the family. The happy household." His eyes lock on mine. "I want it all."

My uterus throbs, my minge pulsing. I'm picturing chiffon and flower girls, sugared roses and a three-tiered buttercream cake from the bakery in Glasgow.

I lean over, kissing him and murmuring against his lips. "Have you ever had sex in a car?"

To which he replies with the most beautiful words. "Any time before you doesn't exist in my memory."

I memorize his words, wanting to write them down, to keep them forever.

This man almost has me ready to plan our wedding.

Almost.

He reaches over me, radiating heat and energy, and pushes a button. I watch as a dark, smoky privacy screen rises between us and the driver.

I shift closer, feeling the heat radiating off him as his hand moves along my thigh, inching my dress higher. The car hums with the low murmur of the engine, creating a deeper sense of privacy in the cab.

His touch ignites a further desire in me, and I can't resist. "I hope you're not planning to take advantage of me in this secluded space," I whisper against his ear, my breath hitching as his fingers trace patterns higher up my inner thigh.

A wicked grin spreads across his face as he leans in, his voice husky with wanton desire. "Who said anything about taking advantage? I believe you wear my ring." His words send a thrill through me, and I bite my lip to suppress a moan. "You belong to me. I can do as I please with you."

Our lips reconnect, igniting a flame of passion between us. His hands roam freely over my body, teasing every inch of skin they touch. I feel the heat between my legs intensify as his fingers dance along my thigh, inching closer to where I ache for his touch the most.

"Tell me what you want," he whispers low against my ear, warm words caressing my skin.

I guide his hand to where I need him most, feeling the anticipation building with each teasing caress. "I want to come."

"And you shall have everything your heart desires." His fingers tease the area just where the tops of my thighs are pressed together, stroking a lazy finger up and down between my thighs. "But to get what you want, first you have to share with me your filthiest fantasy."

Chapter Sixteen

F redrick

"Just when I think you're all historical facts and matching sweaters, you pull out the naughtiest requests," she murmurs.

"I'm those things, too." I brush my lips against hers. "I can be both." With one hand on each of her knees, she responds eagerly to my touch. I slide my hands up her thighs, parting them gently and reveling in the power I have over her. "Tell me," I command, my voice low and husky.

"My fantasy is to be taken by you, here and now, in this car, with no one else around," she whispers, my heart pounding as she speaks. "I want you to touch me everywhere and show me just how much you want me."

I stare into her eyes, cupping her face. "Your wish is my command."

My hand glides slowly along the curve of her breast, the thin fabric of her dress barely a barrier between us. She lets out a soft moan as my fingers playfully tease across her nipple, causing it to harden under my touch.

Moving lower, I trace delicate patterns over her stomach before pausing at the hem of her dress. With a look of pure desire in my eyes, I slowly slide her dress up, revealing more and more of her secret world that belongs only to me.

"You are absolutely breathtaking," I whisper, my breath hitching at the sight of her. Slowly, I lift her dress around her waist, revealing smooth skin and delicate curves. My fingers trail along the edge of her hip. As I near the junction of her thighs, she quivers under my touch, her body betraying her excitement. The anticipation in her eyes is palpable as I tease closer to her most sensitive spot.

"I want to see you," I say. "Take off your panties."

She follows my command, her hands reaching up to her skirt. As she shimmies out of her panties, I can't help but feel a surge of desire. I gently push her legs apart, taking in the sight of her exposed body.

I lean in, whispering against her ear. "Do you trust me?"

"Yes."

"And are you mine?"

"For now."

"Forever," I correct as I begin to explore her with my expert fingers, dipping into her wetness and touching her in all the right places. Her body responds to me instantly, arching her back and closing her eyes in anticipation of this climax.

I pull away, leaving her breathless and exposed. My tone is low, taunting against her ear. "You didn't do as I asked," I chide. "I know you have a dirty fantasy hidden in that pretty little head of yours. Don't be shy." I can sense her hesitation and shame, but it only makes me want to push her further. Force her to open up to me, to reveal secret sexy parts of herself no other man has conquered.

She's quiet for an unlike-Freya amount of time. I begin to think I may have to coax her further, but then she starts to whisper. "You know I was raised a good girl on the island. I longed to be sexy, to dance in a club. A strip club. Wear a sexy dress and tease all the men, wrapping my body around that pole, finally stripping off the dress till I'm wearing nothing but a thong."

Her admission hits me like a wave of hot lava. Gorgeous Freya, my ultimate desire, opening up to me with her secret fantasy. I'm the luckiest man in the world. "Tell me more," I demand, fingering her.

Her voice shakes as she squirms under my touch. "My filthiest fantasy is to be a stripper in the VIP room, dancing for a client who makes me have sex with him."

Her teeth sink into her bottom lip; she stares at me as if waiting for disapproval.

I can handle the fantasy. Of course, I picture myself as this mystery man in the VIP suite—anyone else I would kill. It's my game—I'm happy to play along, turned on by her trust in me. "I can imagine your Freya goddess power. Making men fall at your feet. Tell me more about this fantasy."

She looks as if she can hardly believe what she's about to say. "I would wear a shimmering silver dress and dance for him. I would feel his eyes on me."

She keeps going, my desire growing, fueled by her words. "Then, as the music slows, I would slowly unbutton my dress, revealing more and more of my body until I'm standing before him in just a thong and high heels, topless. My movements would make him want me so badly." The vivid picture she paints makes me want her more.

"I want you. I want you so bad. Every moment of every day." I gently trace circles around her pert nipples. They grow harder under my touch. She gives a shiver and a little gasp. I love how I'm the only man allowed to touch her anywhere, but especially her breasts, knowing she's comfortable with only me. "You're so fucking sexy, Freya. Tell me how it ends..."

"Finally, I would straddle him on the VIP stage and grind against him, showing him just how much he wanted me. He would be helpless against me, unable to resist my temptation." She arches her hips forward. "Touch me there. Please."

I tease her wetness with my fingers, quickly bringing her back to that place of pleasure. Her fingers clutch at the edge of the leather seat; her eyes close, her head presses back. Her hips move around, working with my fingers.

She gasps, speaking in a choked voice as I make her come. "And I crawl over his lap. Put my hands on his—oh my God—shoulders. Sit on his cock and fuuuuuck!" She cries out as she climaxes. "Oh my God, I'm coming!"

I'm desperate to live out her fantasy, my blood hot, my heart pulsing, my cock throbbing. I touch her till she shudders, then quickly unzip my pants, pulling out my erect cock, so ready for this, so turned on by her energy.

Her eyes lock with mine, filled with trust and desire, only fueling my fire. "Come here, princess. Sit on your man. Dance for me, princess."

Putting her hands on my shoulders, she parts her legs, straddling my lap. I lean close to her ear, my voice rough with control. "This is where you dance for only me, Freya." I moan, focused on her warmth as she envelops me, taking every inch as she descends onto me.

My hands firmly grasp her hips, directing her movements as she rides me to pleasure.

Her voice is breathy with lust. "I was picturing you as that man the whole time."

Her eyes meet mine, their intensity igniting a fire within me. "You're such a good woman, Freya. Any man would be lucky to have you dance for him. I thank God it's me." Needing her taste, I thrust my tongue into her mouth.

Her kiss is hungry in return. Her hands grip my shoulders tightly as she moves faster and harder, her moans becoming louder and more desperate, her body trembling. I can tell she's getting close.

I thrust up into her, our bodies moving in sync, fitting together like a puzzle. The moment consumes me, driving me as wild as she described in her fantasy. We continue to make love in the back of the car with the driver on the other side of the partition.

Our kiss softens, then deepens as the climax approaches. My pulse quickens, and my skin grows damp. Each move is synchronized to perfection, each thrust pushing me closer to the edge. The anticipation builds, and with one final push, I cry out her name, feeling the tightness beginning to release. "Freya."

We collide into one another, hard and fast, as we chase that final peak in unison. We are lost in each other's arms, our bodies still connected after the climax, her sitting on my lap, her head nestled in the cradle of my neck. We stay united, enjoying the aftershocks of the mind-blowing sex we just shared.

She murmurs against me. "This," she says. "Was NOT on your itinerary."

Often traveling for work, I ensure my car is fully stocked with self-care items. We're easily able to reassemble ourselves for the day. I clean her body with damp cloths and we straighten our clothing. Spritzing a lavender-scented spray in the cab, I leave the rest to the driver.

When we arrive at the Royal Mile, we exit the car and follow my security team till they fan out into the crowds, giving us the space she requested.

Drunk on afterglow, heady with cold air and sunshine, I bring up a subject I've left marinating. "You want children as well."

"Aye. Not now, of course. But one day," she says.

I can't describe the feeling I get when she says she wants children—like a warm liquid ray of sunshine easing over me. I've never experienced this before.

Not only do we want the same thing, but if she's to be a mother, her dangerous career will be a distant memory. My children will want for nothing. They will have everything I didn't.

Most importantly, they will have a loving mother.

Why wait?

My protective hand goes to her lower back, thinking of a past conversation we had, one where she very clearly told me she is taking oral contraception. "Let's get you off the pill now. I want to put a baby in that belly tonight."

She snorts. "It doesn't work like that! You have to plan; it takes weeks, and I'm nowhere near ready to get off that pill. I went on it at sixteen to clear my skin and have no plans of going off it now."

"How long will you wait? Time is ticking."

She narrows her gaze, peering up at me. "Are you calling me old?"

"No, but aren't the eggs healthier when young?"

"Since when are you so interested in women's fertility?" She's clearly annoyed. "I'm sure my eggs are just fine, thank you."

"Well, when the time comes, we both agree; you will stay home."

"Having me locked up in Inverness, under your watchful eye 24/7, is your filthy fantasy, isn't it?" she says.

"Oui. I like to know you're safe."

"I will marry first, then have children, and then return to law."

"And does your partner get any say in the matter?" I ask, thinking of my upbringing. I do not want the same for my children.

She grabs my hand, giving it a gentle squeeze.

Her voice softens. "I understand your pain. I promise I do. What happened to you should never happen to a child. Of course, it would make you want your wee ones to have their mother at their beck and call. But children can have love, support, and all those wonderful things and still have two working parents."

What she says next fills me with hope.

She gives a shy smile, one I've not seen on her pretty face before. "We'd have Fiona and Morven and the staff to help us. Hopefully, everything will be cleared by then, and friends and family will surround us."

She. Said. We.

We. Us. Her and I.

"You said we." I grin. "You were talking about us."

"Of course! We're engaged." She holds up a hand, letting her diamond ring glitter in the sun.

Her matter-of-fact answer brings me more joy. "It's just that you don't typically speak that way, directly about us."

"Do I not?" Her brow furrows as she thinks. "It's been a confusing journey. You've given me time and patience. I accepted your ring. I should talk in terms of us, and we. Oui?"

Once, I thought I'd drag her down the aisle. Force her to marry me. I had it all wrong.

I agree happily, a breath of relief filling my lungs. "Oui."

"I apologize if I hurt you." She gives my hand a second squeeze. "And I thank you for your patience." She pulls us to a stop on the sidewalk, guards coming to a stop in the corner of my eyes, hovering around us, on the lookout for trouble. Putting her hands on my chest, she gazes up at me. "I will marry you soon, Fredrick Frisque. When the time is right."

Other than her accepting my ring, this is the first confirmation the wedding is coming in my lifetime. My chest wells with hope for our bright future together. I need to lock this down. "When will that be?"

"When things are back to normal, and I can have my family there as witnesses," she says, tears in her eyes.

Of course, she wants a dream wedding, with friends and family overflowing at the ceremony. Me? I'd be happy with only the two of us present, Joyeux as ring bearer.

I kiss her cheek. "I understand."

Satisfied with our breakthrough, I let the conversation lie there, knowing she's been pushed enough for one day. I let her calm her emotions so we can enjoy this day.

The sun shines on our faces. Not knowing if she'd packed sunglasses in our haste to leave, I grabbed her favorite pair from where they sat on the table in the foyer. I slip her cat-eyed Chanel's from the inside pocket of my suit jacket. "Grabbed these for you on the way out the door." I hand them to her.

"Och! You have thought of everything!" She dons the sunglasses, looking adorable in them. "Thank you."

I slide on my own Ray Bans, enjoying the walk and the architecture. I spot my security in their six-point formation around us, but as she suggested, having some space to be a part of the crowd is pleasant.

I try to live in the moment, to let this be enough, but one discrepancy between our thinking tugs at the back of my mind, prickly and uncomfortable. I take a risk, hoping not to ruin our day, but I know I can't focus until I clear this up.

"I do think the woman should stay home with the children."

She waits a beat, then pauses her steps, lifting her glasses to meet my eye. Her lashes flutter. "Have you ever thought about staying home with the children? Plenty of fathers make terrific stay-at-home dads." Point made, she snaps her glasses back down.

"Ma chérie! I'm a man."

"Trust me," she says, eyeing my crotch. "I'm well aware."

"My job is to provide for my family. Protect my family. Guide my children. Support my wife."

"And a woman can do the same for her family." She picks up her pace, eager to end the conversation, briskly moving toward our destination. "Don't let this cause conflict between us. Let's not ruin our day. We still have matching sweaters to purchase."

I grab her hand, attempting to slow her down. "It's an important conversation, Freya. You can't keep pushing everything that makes you uncomfortable away. It will resurface. Best to face it head on."

She tugs me along, keeping her pace brisk. "And I say, best not to ruin our day. There's a time and place for hard conversations, and this is not that time."

I pull her to a stop, forcing her to face me. "It's never the time with you, Freya."

Our gazes lock, fire and ice.

"I don't know why it's so important to you to figure out our future right now." She flips her hair over her shoulder, her defense mechanism. "It's not as if we're married yet."

If it were up to me, we'd have wed when she first walked into the castle. Frustrated, I say, "You wear my ring. You've confirmed your consent. A moment ago, you told me we'd marry soon."

"And we will," she stresses.

I've given her space, time, and understanding. Perhaps too much so. What she needs is to be told, to be dominated, like those seventy castle steps we'll soon undertake; the woman needs to be conquered.

I pull her to a stop, forcing her to face me. "We will be married. You will be my wife. And you will stay home with our children."

She tosses back her head, hair glittering in the sun, and laughs.

Chapter Seventeen

F reya

Though cold, the sun is out, making for a glorious crisp day. I'm still shocked I got him to consent to allowing us to walk this mile. Of course, a little Freya magic helped.

While getting dressed this morning, I conducted some research, tearing a page out of a local travel magazine. Hoping it would sway him, I handed the printout to him as we pulled away from the castle. Timing was part of my earlier caffeine-inspired plan; that way, he wouldn't have too much time to overthink.

"Look!" I pressed brightly. "We have to walk the Royal Mile ourselves, with guards scattered around us, of course. Driving up to the castle will not do. It's not the true tourist experience."

"Walk? Hmm..." His brow is knitted in a firm no.

I pushed the glossy magazine page into his hands. "Here. Read this before you decide. Ken?"

He took the paper, scanning the words.

The Royal Mile, spanning 1.81 km and linking the iconic Edinburgh Castle to the majestic Palace of Holyroodhouse, is a happening hangout spot in the heart of Edinburgh's Old Town. As you stroll down its cobblestone lanes, you'll come across all sorts of cool stuff just waiting to be discovered:

You've got the impressive St Giles' Cathedral, standing tall and proud like a history buff whose intricate architecture tells tales of days gone by.

But wait, there's more! Underneath the bustling street lies The Real Mary King's Close, a hidden world full of twisty alleys and snaking staircases that spill secrets from ancient times.

Feeling fancy? Head to the Scottish Storytelling Centre to get lost in tales of dragons and knights and maybe even a modern-day legend or two.

And don't forget about the sleek and modern Scottish Parliament building - a far cry from the traditional buildings but representing the city's hip and trendy vibe.

While cars are still allowed on this road, it's mostly meant for leisurely strolling, so ditch your wheels and take in all the sights and sounds on foot.

Trust us, it's dead brilliant this way!

THE ARTICLE WAS A LITTLE CHEESY, BUT AS HE read, his brow eased. Craving a little freedom after being restricted to the grounds of Wee Inverness, I crossed my fingers as he returned the paper, saying he was intrigued and would chat with security. I gave him a pre-emptive thank you kiss on the cheek for good measure.

Now, walking the Royal Mile together, hand in hand, the sun warming my icy cheeks, I can't hold back my beaming smile. I'm a perfectly dressed tourist in my own country, with a handsome, frisky man at my side.

Crowds surround us on the street as we gather at the end of the sidewalk to cross over and reach the steep, curving cobblestone road leading us to the brown-and-gray stone castle.

A man stands opposite, facing us from the side of the road to which we are waiting to cross. My eyes pick him out of the crowd because of the toddler he holds. Her hair is dark, almost black—the opposite of mine. In contrast to her dark hair, her skin is porcelain.

The man seems jittery, bouncing the girl on his hip as he stares at the crowd of us waiting opposite him. His eyes are steady and calculating. He spots something, seemingly just behind me.

His face drains of color. I snap my head over my shoulder to see what he's looking at, but it's only a crowd of faces. I turn back to him to find his face filled with fear.

I want a better look. I perch my sunglasses on top of my head. His gaze lands on mine.

My heart lurches into my throat. His eyes are pale blue. Ice blue. Too light. Only then do I see the dark vine tattoo creeping up the side of his neck.

The man from the club.

Fredrick stands beside me, unaware of any of this, grumbling something to himself about crowds.

"It's him." My voice comes out in a whisper. I tug Fredrick's hand, raising my voice. "The man from Level Z."

He instantly focuses. "Where?"

"There, across the street. The one with the light blue eyes and the vine tattoo on his neck. The one the bartender took away."

He pushes a button at his ear, informing the guards of what I've seen, saying a name I've never heard: Ross Macdonald. He waits for a beat, listening for their instructions, then says, "They say move forward. They've spotted two members of the Hoax just behind us. They don't think they have any idea we're here. They think they are here for Ross."

Fredrick's hand presses protectively against my lower back. I think of that night when he tried to speak to me, and the bartender whisked him away. What did he want to tell me?

Now, the crowd is pushing against us, an unstoppable flow of migrating pack animals heading straight to him.

I feel safe with Fredrick and his team, his arm wrapping around my shoulders as we move. I don't take my eyes off the man. Ross Macdonald only stops staring at me long enough to whisper down to the baby, kissing her head before focusing back on me.

He's almost upon us. The way he's staring at me with such intention, I can't imagine what he wants from me. What do I do? "Do we just keep walking?"

"Yes. We must act relaxed and continue on our path to avoid

bringing attention to ourselves. The guards have us covered."

I wait for the man to pass me, but instead, so quickly neither Fredrick nor I can react, the man presses his heat and weight against me, then is gone from our sight.

And in my arms...

A dark-haired baby stares up at me, confusion in her island sky-blue eyes. Holding her light, warm weight against my chest, I realize she's smaller and younger than I first thought.

Fredrick's voice echoes around me. "What on Earth? Where has he gone?"

I can't stop in the middle of the street, so I keep moving.

In my shock, my body reacts on its own. I wrap my arms tighter around the child, shifting her weight to hold her as securely as possible. I smooth her hair, whispering to her, "It's okay. Everything is going to be okay."

"What in the world?" Fredrick says again. We're on the sidewalk now, our guards surrounding us. The men quickly usher us off the sidewalk and back to the road, where there's a waiting Escalade.

They start to usher me and the baby into the back seat. I hover outside the door to glance around. "Wait! Where's her father?"

Fredrick puts a hand on my shoulder, wanting me to get in the SUV. "He's being pursued by two men we identified as members of the Hoax."

"Should we help him?" I stare down at the beauty in my arms. "He is her father."

"No. Absolutely not. I will not put you in danger." His eyes shift to the street. "We haven't even decided if we should take the girl."

She chooses this moment to stare up at me, giving me a tiny smile. So young. A wee bit older than a year?

"Not take her with us? I'm still trying to figure out how to save her father."

"We need to do what security deems best for you." He hovers around me, one hand on me, the other on top of the car's door, creating a protective cocoon around me and the baby while he waits for confirmation.

"We're absolutely taking her with us." Acting as her armor, I curve my body around her tiny one, sliding us into the safety of the back seat of the Escalade. Without arguing, Fredrick scans the road around us, then follows suit, sitting beside me.

His hand is on the handle of the car door, ready to close it, when we hear the gunshot. The noise is distant yet undeniable. Gasps and shouts from the street follow the terrifying sound.

The baby, blissfully unaware, quickly adapts to her surroundings. She tugs on the end of my scarf, intrigued by its soft cashmere fringe.

The door is closed, and the Escalade pulls from the curb.

My heart lunges into my throat. Her father is dead. "That... was him."

"More than likely." Fredrick wraps his arm around my shoulders, pulling me tight against his side. He offers me the strength I do not have as I hold this precious life in my arms, knowing her entire world has been destroyed at this moment.

I force myself not to react, smiling down at the baby as tears sting my eyes. To my side, I catch Fredrick making the quiet motions of the sign of the cross, kissing his fingertips as he finishes, then glancing up at heaven.

He's praying for her father.

The tears well.

The baby looks up at me, eyeing the strands of shiny pearls I wear around my neck. Gleefully, she gently tugs on the necklace, blissfully unaware of what's happening around us as she purses her rosebud lips, soundlessly blowing bubbles.

She has no idea...

I quickly wipe a tear from my cheek. "Aren't you a clever girl?"

She's so quiet, not even jumping at the sound of the gun. Something flips in my gut; I feel off-center, prickly heat dancing over the back of my neck. "She can't hear."

"What do you mean?" Fredrick asks.

Traffic starts back up, and we pull forward, the car lurching forward as the driver accelerates.

"Gunshots. Mayhem on the street, and look." I nod at the baby, who playfully blows bubbles, fingertips now at her rosy lips. "She's serene. She hasn't made a sound."

Studying her face, he leans forward, his arm shifting but remaining on my shoulder as he takes his fingers to her ear and snaps. Twice. The baby looks at him and laughs.

Relieved she reacted to the sound of his snapping, I push his hand away. "Don't do that! She's not a dog."

"It's a simple test. And it worked. I wanted to put your mind at ease." His arm slides away from my shoulder. "I'm pragmatic."

We sit there in silence, in shock, and let the weight of the gunshot sink in.

Staring down at the sweet girl, I stroke her silky hair. "We should have gone back."

"Absolutely not." His voice is tight. "I'll never willingly put you in danger."

My hackles rise. "But what about the wee one? She's got no father now."

"If we'd gone back for the father who, for all intents and purposes..." His voice trails off as he stares at the baby. There's compassion in his voice. "He was already gone. We could have put her in more danger."

As he said, he's pragmatic. He snapped his fingers because it was the quickest way to ease my mind. And the silent prayer...I've always had a soft spot for a strong man turning to God in a moment of weakness.

I tell my anger to cool itself.

"You're right, Fredrick, we couldn't go back. I'm sorry." I lean my head on his shoulder. "Thank you for your protection."

"Ma chérie." He kisses the top of my head. "Don't apologize. If you didn't want to try and save him, you wouldn't be you."

"It's the islander in me. Leave no one behind." Only they left me, didn't they? I stare down at the baby, my pain tripling for her.

Together, we stare at the precious little girl as she tires. Slowly, her body weight increases, and her breathing slows. Her wee head rests on my chest, using my down coat as a pillow. Her thick lashes flutter. A moment later, she's fast asleep.

I have no idea how to care for a child. I wasn't like Fiona or the other girls on the island, babysitting loads of little cousins when their mothers had things to attend to or a knitting circle.

I was always out. Rolling my uniform skirt up higher and smoking ciggies behind the school. Or riding on the back of the motorcycle of the town's "bad boy," Bayne, who at the time happened to be my brother's arch nemesis but is now happily married.

Or I was getting older kids to buy me alcohol until I was finally the older kid and could take the bus down to the closest thing that passed for an actual town and party at the pubs.

With Callum only being fifteen months my junior, we were more like twins rather than having the typical older-younger sibling relationship.

Even if I don't know what I'm doing, I instantly connect to this little girl.

I commit to myself and her that I will figure it out, that as long as she's in our care, we will provide for her every need. Now, this little girl is my priority.

As far as the wedding, the renovations, and the ongoing friction between Fredrick and me, as my grandma used to say, it'll keep.

There are more pressing issues at hand.

Like figuring out her name, who she is, where she comes from, and God and my poor little heart forbid—finding other family members to give her back to.

If we do find them, will they be a part of the terrible people-trafficking ring, the Hoax? Will she be safe? There's no way Ross could have known I would be there today, that I would cross that sidewalk at that moment.

Has fate brought us this wee precious girl?

Chapter Eighteen

Fredrick

THE MOMENT I SAW FREYA, I HAD TO HAVE HER.

When her brother worried about her safety, I knew I could be the husband she needed, give her the world, and protect her. And I would have what I wanted and needed, and she would be mine.

No heartstrings attached.

The vision of beautiful Freya, fiercely protective of a child in her arms, instantly shifts my reality. I no longer care about what I want. The wedding can wait. The only thing that matters is Freya and the girl in her arms.

Speaking with my security, I found we couldn't insulate the incident from public knowledge. Things were already complicated for Freya after representing Jack. Now, being handed a baby by a member of the Hoax in broad daylight just before the man's execution, the islander's tongues will be wagging.

We don't know if the two men from the Hoax saw him hand Freya the baby or if they have any interest in pursuing the little one. We need more information. "We must meet with the Kings, face to face, and decide how to move forward."

"I was thinking the same." Her green eyes blaze bravely. "We'll go to Norse Garden. Direct the driver there, now."

"I have, and I'll send word to Callum to have as many Kings there as possible." He had been distant on the phone, most likely confused by Freya's further interaction with the Hoax.

"Ask Fiona to gather the things the baby will need for now —diapers, clothing." I check a tag in her clothing, telling Fredrick her size. "What do babies her age eat? Fiona will know."

"Security cleared us for this meeting." I think of the pain and tension between her and her family. "Are you sure you're ready to go back there?"

"I love Callum and Fiona. I trust my brother with my life. And yours, and hers. I'm one of the Kings; they've vowed to protect me. As for the rumors? Small towns have more upsides than not, but I cannae deny my lovely wee island suffers from gossip. I no longer care what people think of me. For the moment, we need to be in Glasgow with the Kings to figure this out. I'll not put this baby in harm's way." Her voice breaks. "Pearl has already lost her father."

"Pearl?"

She shakes her head. "I can't keep calling her girl and wee one. She deserves a nickname until we find out who she is."

"Of course." I run a finger over the baby's round cheek, feeling its baby softness. "Pearl because she plays with your necklace?"

"She likes my necklace so much…and it's silly, but with her luminescent skin and dark hair, her face is like a little pearl, encapsulated in a dark oyster shell." She gives me a pensive look. "Have your men had any luck tracking down information on the father? Ross Macdonald, you called him?"

"Yes, the Kings know him as Ross Macdonald. As with any of the other members with a previous criminal record, he was given a new identity when he joined the Hoax, so it will take some time to find his given name. The Kings are tracking down information on the mother and any other blood relatives they can find. It isn't easy. The Hoax is very good at covering their tracks."

"Do we know why he wanted to speak to me at the club that night?" She peers down at little Pearl, smiling as the little one gives a content sigh in her sleep, nestling deeper against Freya's chest.

"There are a few theories our informants have put together. Some think he was trying to leave the Hoax. He'd heard you'd represented Jack Maclean and knew you didn't make the connection. One theory is that he thought you could help him somehow."

Her eyes widen. "From what the Kings know so far, they think Ross seeing me on the street today was random?"

"They think he was running away, right then, right there. And he was being followed. That it was fate that made our paths cross at that moment. He saw you and either trusted you or was desperate and, recognizing you, handed her off for her safety."

She shakes her head, whispering, "Kismet."

"Seems to be." I don't believe in fate. Now is not the time to start another disagreement between us.

"Gah. What will people say now?" She glances at me, steeling her nerves. "You know what—I don't care. I don't freck—stinking care."

We sit quietly for a moment. She rests her head on the back of the headrest, closing her eyes, privately diving into her thoughts, most likely mentally preparing herself to face everyone after all this time and trauma.

Fiona and Callum greet us at the door. After a quick round of greetings and reluctantly handing Pearl off to Fiona, Freya and I sit side by side on one end of the long table in the Great Hall, ready to work.

Only Callum joins us. I want to ask where the other members of the Kings are.

I don't.

Either distracted by her need to protect Pearl first or too overwhelmed to notice the empty room, Freya's first question is, "What's everyone saying about what happened today?"

"The stories are so ridiculous, I'd laugh if I weren't so angry about them." Callum runs a hand over his beard.

"Tell me your favorite," Freya demands dryly.

He winces. "You've been with the Hoax since the age of sixteen, acting as an informant for them, spilling the secrets of the Kings."

"Och! No!" Freya says.

"It gets better," Callum says. "The baby you've brought here—"

I interject on Freya's behalf. "We'll call her Pearl for now." Freya shoots me a grateful look as her brother continues.

Callum adopts the new name. "Pearl—Pearl Macdonald—a love child of Freya and Ross. Even though Freya's figure could never be described as anything other than 'willowy.'"

"People are ridiculous. I should know. I'm the queen of petty gossip." She quickly looks at me, adding, "I mean, I used to be. In my younger days."

Callum continues, "Hence, Pearl inherits Freya's pale skin. Freya has had to hide Pearl until now in her attempt to remain an undercover member of the Hoax."

"Why would I expose Pearl now?" Freya asks.

"Ross was going to defect. That part is true. Knowing he was in trouble, you lovers planned this handoff," Callum explains.

"Careful there. Choose another word," I groan.

"There's one you might like better, then, Fredrick. One that is a wee bit closer to Ross's truth."

"Lay it on us," Freya says.

"Ross did want to leave the Hoax. He must have known about the few other members we've trusted enough to take into our fold. I think he wanted to talk to Freya to see if it was possible to bring him aboard. In return, he would help you by telling everyone the truth; you were targeted and knew nothing of Jack's involvement in the Hoax."

"I like that one best." Freya nods. "Everyone else has decided what is true without sticking to facts. I'll do the same. I choose that story to be the real one."

"And what part do I play in all these legends?"

Callum offers me his grin. "You're her henchman. You do her bidding. Blinded by Freya's beauty and blissfully unaware of her traitorous nature."

"Nice." Freya turns to me. "Though I do like the idea of bossing you around."

I shoot her a stern look. Turning the conversation, I ask, "Have they found the mother?"

I feel Freya bristle beside me at the question.

"Not yet." Folding his arms on the table, Callum shakes his head. "We've no idea who she is or her whereabouts, nor will we till we find Ross's birthname."

"She could be gone," Freya offers.

"Or, scared of Ross and in hiding. Hopefully, we will find the mam and the wee one's family. It's best for all parties involved if the baby returns to the mother and the Kings close this chapter."

For everyone but Freya, I can't help but think. She's grown too attached, too fast. Losing the little girl to an uncertain future will be difficult after the trauma bonding they've done today.

Freya eyes her brother, asking the question I know has been on her mind. "Where are we on the Jack Maclean case?"

"There has been a wee bit of good news in that department." Too quickly, Callum adds, "And a hard truth as well."

I glance over at Freya. She looks as if she's frozen. I wrap my arm around her shoulders, pulling her closer and warming her.

I say, "Good news first."

"Part of the Ross theory you liked must be true because before he disappeared, word did get around from someone on their side that you were a target, that they knew your close connections were with the elder Mr. Maclean, and you didn't know about Jack."

"Thank God." She collapses against me. "That is good news."

My heart sinks as I guess what's coming next. I tighten my hold around her. Callum forces himself to meet his sister's gaze. "Freya..."

She straightens. "Callum. Come out with it."

He strokes that beard like it's his only comfort. "I don't know how to say this—"

She narrows her gaze, her courtroom voice coming out. "Just say it then. Please."

He shakes his head. "The Kings have taken a vote. We cannae longer risk having you in the inner circle."

Now I understand the empty room.

I've heard the whispers. I felt this vote coming. Still, I'm in disbelief that the family could turn her out of their inner workings.

My voice booms through the hall. "I didn't get a vote."

Callum locks eyes with me, sadness in his voice. "We dinnae need it, brother. The numbers were unanimous." His Burnes green eyes return to Freya's. "Save for mine."

The deafening quiet of tension fills the vast space.

Finally, Freya breaks the silence. She passes her hand over the table, placing it over Callum's. "I thank ye for that, brother."

"You'll still have the Kings' support and protection, of course. We will never break our vow. In time, things will blow over. Your name will be cleared, Freya. Thanks to Ross, it's already begun." He flips his hand over, grabbing hers tight. "You know I'll always trust ye, Freya. With my life."

"Same." She gives him a sad, brave smile. "Always."

I know her heart is breaking, but she straightens her posture, steadies her tone, and says, "We'd best be on our way." Pushing her chair back, she stands. I join her.

"We'll just grab Pearl and be on our way—" She looks up at me, her eyes locking on mine. "On our way home."

Her final word hangs in the air: home, a beautiful sound. She's officially accepting Wee Inverness as her place of belonging and me as her person, leaving Norse Garden Estates behind. Gratitude washes over me—Freya and me, against the world. Or, better yet, nestled in our own little world that we've both come to love, offering one another the comfort and acceptance we so desperately need.

"Let's go home." I lean down, kissing her lips.

Callum breaks the moment. "That'd be best. Unfortunately,

the Kings cannae offer protection to a child of a member of the Hoax."

At the mention of Pearl, Freya goes warrior. "Even when her father was executed? A refugee, given no hope."

Still a loyal leader of the Kings, Callum answers her with a solid, "Aye."

"Even if it's a wee one we're talking about protecting?" Freya crosses her arms over her chest, darting him her "big sister" stare. I've seen her use it on Callum before.

This time, Callum doesn't waver. "Aye, Freya. It's not possible."

He rounds the table to take Freya in his arms. "I'm sorry—"

"Stop." She quickly rises on tiptoe, kissing his cheek before pushing him onto me for goodbyes so she can wipe the tears from her eyes privately.

His gaze meets mine as he gives me a firm handshake. "I know you'll take care of them both."

"With my life," I say.

Callum says, "I'll be in touch." We embrace briefly before leaving the room to collect Pearl and say goodbye to Fiona.

My future with the Kings was not discussed tonight, nor do I care to.

My loyalty lies with Freya. If Freya is out of the inner circle, I will also extract myself. We are a package deal. We leave the Great Hall, and she holds my hand tightly.

She knows my thoughts. "Thanks for always being at my side."

I give her hand a reassuring squeeze. It was so lovely to hear her say the words. I ask her, "Freya, tell me, where are we going?"

"Home, Fredrick. Let's go home." She gives my hand a return squeeze.

After a tearful goodbye between her and Fiona, we leave, Pearl sleeping in her arms. She's quiet on the ride home, her face trained at the window. She's lost her community, now her place in the Kings. Soon, she will lose that precious baby in her arms, as well.

Freya's strength first drew me to her; as I said, she's a sword, and I'm more than happy to be her shield. Even a goddess warrior has an Achilles heel, hers being the love of her people. Even with those ties healing, Freya has her breaking point.

I fear we're growing dangerously close to that line.

Chapter Nineteen

Freya

A FEW WEEKS AGO, IN THE MIDDLE OF THAT STREET in Edinburgh, I held that little girl in my arms, shielding her from the world, and instantly, she felt like mine.

But och!—how fate has done me wrong!

Does she adore me? Yes. She gives me her sunshine-filled smile the moment I walk in the door. She reaches her wee arms out for me to pick her up.

But when she's hurt, scared, and feels like there is anything just a little bit off in her world...

She wants *him*.

I'd say it's infuriating, but any woman with a uterus knows the flutters you feel when a handsome, stoic man melts under the tender weight of a child, soothing them with sweet words. A carnal power as old as the Earth takes over.

You want to ride him hard and fill your empty womb with his babies.

I know, eventually, we will find Pearl's family and reunite them.

We're doing all we can to find her mother and blood relatives. It's been weeks without so much as a nibble. There are no missing children's reports that match her unique description, and there are no files that Social Care Support or Child Protective Committees can find with a photo like hers. A DNA test did find us one match; her father had one done when he was in police custody a few years ago.

Ross Macdonald is an alias. The dead man with the light blue eyes and vine tattoo on his neck, Pearl's father, is really Tartan Erwin—a thirty-four-year-old Scottish man with prior domestic violence convictions.

After searching the National Records of Scotland for any birth registered in Scotland since 1855, we've not found his unique first name, Tartan, listed as a father on any extracts, or short or full birth certificates.

Regardless, as any solicitor knows, DNA doesn't lie.

He's undoubtedly Pearl's father. Though Erwin is a fairly common surname, it at least gave us a reasonable avenue to begin the search, but it's possible the mother gave the child her last name, not his, at birth.

We've picked up a few names from the clubs and bars, women Erwin possibly could have connected with. We'll follow every lead. With the new information, we should close in soon.

My wee heart can't process the thought of her leaving our

home. Often, these days, I say, "*Vivre l'instant present*. Live in the present moment."

I've been learning French and everything there is to know about infants, Pearl in particular. I've been learning about her favorite foods, naptimes and bedtimes, and how she gets angry if she misses a single meal or snack. She eats six times daily, a girl after my own grazing heart. We've taken her to the pediatrician, the dentist, and many therapy sessions.

With everything she's been through, I want her to have her best foot forward when she is reunited with her family.

I tell myself to enjoy my time with her, to live in the present, to forgive the Kings and the islanders who doubt me, and to move on with my future.

Fredrick. My perfect match. My new family.

He's given me so much, and it's time for me to give him what he wants more than anything in Scotland's green hills —a wedding. Complete with the sweetest wee flower girl.

I've been preparing for the last two weeks.

It's time to implement the plan. I handwrite an invitation using the calligraphy lettering Fiona taught me in her art studio at Norse Garden. When I'm finished, the words look like Pearl or Happy may have drawn them, but the information is all there.

She claps her wee hands. "Tit-ty, tit-ty!"

"KIT-ty," I say, emphasizing the K sound. "That's right. Mr. Happy Halloween is coming over to check you out."

Pearl claps her hands as Happy creeps over slowly, whiskers twitching as he checks her out. So far, he's been very unsure of Pearl, with good reason.

She laughs her belly laugh and goes right for his tail. "Titty!"

"No, no. Don't pull his tail. Here. Help me with my card." I redirect Pearl's attention, handing her a red crayon. She immediately puts it in her mouth. I take it from her, getting a clean purple one. I hold it up to her, saying, "PUR-PLE. We like this color better anyway. Let me show you. Like this."

Soon, she's scribbling happily, and Happy can make his escape.

When the invitation is truly a beautiful mess, I hold Pearl on my hip, and she proudly holds the paper up. "Let's go find Fredrick!"

He's in the kitchen. Morven is trying to show him how to boil noodles. They both stand at the gas stove, staring into a pot. Fredrick grabs an open box of bow ties from the counter, ready to pour them in. Morven taps the counter with the wooden spoon in her hand. "You don't put the pasta in until the water is boiling."

"Oooh," he says. "I had no idea. No wonder mine never comes out right."

Morven tsks, shaking her head good-naturedly. I clear my throat, announcing our presence. Fredrick and Morvan turn to greet us, both their faces lighting up.

"What have you got there for me, little Pearl?" Fredrick asks.

She hands him the card.

Morven steps in. "Here, let me take the baby. It's bathtime."

"Thank you, Morven." I flash her an excited grin.

Morven gives me a wink as she takes Pearl in her arms. She's in on my plan.

Fredrick's eyes follow Morven's retreat, aghast. "Wait! Who's going to make the pasta?"

Morven chuckles. "You supermodels will figure it out. Surely you two aren't just pretty faces."

I walk over, turn the knob, and cut the gas. "We'll order out."

"Thank God. That was intense. I really can't cook." He looks down at the invite. "Pretty. Are you teaching Pearl to hog up the purple crayon as well?"

My excitement bubbles to the surface. The wait is killing me. "Read it!"

His features soften as he reads the words. He glances up at me, then back at the invite, as if he's making sure it's real. His eyes make my heart and womb do that fluttering thing.

Finally, he says, "Are you sure? You said you wanted to wait till you had your family here with us."

"Aye." I nod. "It would make me very happy to become your wife." I stare up at him. "Would it make you happy?"

"Oui. Absolutely." He cups my face with his hand, kissing me deeply. My knees go weak, my heart flitter-fluttering.

"Like the invite says, please join us in the garden at seven pm sharp." Morven storms into the room at the sound of my words, making a beeline for me. She pulls me away from Fredrick. "Excuse us a moment, sir."

Fredrick gives me a curious look as Morven whispers into my ear. "I gave the baby to the nurse so I could call hubby and be sure he's going to have our delivery. The angel has NOT landed. I repeat, the angel has NOT landed. He needs more time to get it right. He's not even coming tonight." She rolls her eyes. "Artists. They can't be controlled, ken?"

If we can't have her, the garden doesn't seem like the right place for our nuptials.

I go into event planner mode, pulling Morven deeper into the butler pantry. "Let's have the staff set up in the ballroom instead."

"Great idea!" she whisper-shouts. "My idea in the first place. You never know what the Scotland skies will surprise you with. Let me go; the next hour will be hoachin'!" She rushes off to make the last-minute changes.

I return to Fredrick, laughing at the curious look on his face. "Nothing you need to worry yourself over, honey. Wear your black Armani tux, please."

"And you wear that gorgeous dress that looks so stunning." He pulls me into him. "I lost my breath the first time I saw you in that gown."

My gorgeous one-of-a-kind gown that was made just for me. I no longer care when it was made or how long ago Callum planned for me to come under Fredrick's wing. I only care about looking as beautiful as he makes me feel and saying my vows.

Where's my dress!

The morning after I arrived, he had the gown neatly hung in my closet. I moved it to one of his wardrobes. Thus began a daily tug-of-war power game, with the dress now having been in every closet of this castle.

My blood chills—no dress, no wedding. I have no time to search every closet. I've been reduced to repeating hiding spots, my memory muddled on where I put it today. The only day that matters.

He saves the day. "I found your dress in the pastry cupboard this morning. There's a spray of flour on it that I had to dust off, but otherwise, it's safely back in your closet."

Whew! Close one. "As you do every day." I wrap my arms around his neck and kiss him. "I can always count on you."

He scoops his hands around my ass, squeezing tight. "But move it out of our closet after tonight, and you'll be back over my lap."

The heat warms me everywhere, his hands on my ass, making me want to beg him to spank and fuck me right here, right now, in this kitchen. I gather up my weak self-control, reminding myself I have a wedding to throw.

"You stop that. This is going to be a classy event. We don't need your frisky ways, Mr. Frisque." I pull away.

He grabs both of my hands, pulling me back into him. "Mrs. Frisky Frisque. Finally."

He's kissing me and won't let me go. Finally, I tear myself away to get ready. "Don't be late."

The staff that helped me with my makeup and hair that first night now aid me again. We chat and laugh this time like the friends we've become, while I share strawberries and champagne with the group.

I wore dangling earrings since I was going to do my hair up, but everyone made me blush with compliments, telling me that with hair like mine, it has to stay down. They're helping me with the final touch, latching the strap of my sparkling gown. There's a knock at the door.

Morven lets herself in. "Just me, just me. I can't let the groom see his bride before the vows. It's bad luck, so I've come to deliver the gift myself."

"A gift from Fredrick?" I ask.

"Aye! A lovely one, I must say. Sure to be your new best friend," Morven laughs.

"New best friend! Is it a puppy?" I tease. "Have you finally relented, Morven? Can we have a dog?"

"NO! Ack! No way. Happy is enough fur to hoover." Her face wrinkles as she pictures the muddy paw prints in the spring I've heard so many horror stories about. She reaches into her apron pocket, pulls out the silver foil, and pops her allergy pill in her mouth. I hand her a glass of champagne. Gratefully she accepts, washing down the pill with a swallow. "Something better than a messy puppy."

She hands me a large, flat jewelry box. The staff gathers around, peering over my shoulder to see what's inside. I flip open the lid, instantly blinded as light hits diamond.

With the dress's high neckline, the necklace is a stunning work of art that will rest just below my collarbone. An asymmetrical design, three tear-drop-shaped pieces, growing in size as they move to the side, each studded with brilliant diamonds. The earrings match perfectly, with three teardrops increasing in size as they waterfall down.

The pieces must be collectively encrusted in thousands of diamonds.

Holy Green Hills of Scotland. The man has robbed the Crown Jewels. I stare into the box, breathless. "This cannot be for me."

Sabrina, here only for the night, says, "Oh, girl, there ain't no other woman in Inverness those diamonds are meant for. Let me put those on you before one of these thirsty gals steals them and runs you off the altar." She leans over, closing the clasp of the necklace.

I stare in the mirror and feel lovely. I thank everyone, accepting their careful hugs as they congratulate me without wrinkling the dress. I wonder when he could have bought the jewelry, and like the engagement ring, I let it be his secret.

Morven escorts me downstairs.

As I enter the ballroom, I am struck by its transformation. Our renovations gave the wood a gleaming shine and the white walls a pristine condition. The grand space was empty but has now been dressed up for the ceremony.

My matron of honor and witness, Morven, squeezes my arm in triumph. "Told you!" she whispers in my ear.

"You were right," I reply, in awe of the scene before me. Twinkling lights and gauzy tulle drape from the rafters, creating a dreamlike atmosphere. Lavender ribbons hang in broad arcs, tied in large, elegant bows. White paper bags line the floor, weighed down with sand and filled with battery-operated candles. Their gentle glow leads toward a simple arch adorned with the same sparkling tulle and ribbons. At the end of the aisle stands the Frisque family's minister, who has traveled from France to officiate our ceremony.

The same man who performed Fredrick's mother's funeral. I thought having some connection to her today would be good for him.

I take a deep breath, feeling emotionally overwhelmed as I walk toward the arch. This is the moment I have been fighting against for months with him, then had weeks of daydreaming about it. Now, I can hardly believe that it is happening.

As I reach the arch to wait for my soon-to-be husband, I can't help but give Morven a parting smile, silently thanking her. She was right—this was the perfect space for our ideal moment.

The minister extends his hand for a handshake; I feel my nerves build up. "Mademoiselle," he says with a charming smile.

My giggle betrays my unease, the weight of his words suddenly sinking in. "Madame Frisque soon... I suppose." My mind reels with the implications.

He reassures me with a kind smile. "A lovely Mrs. Frisque you will be."

"Thank ye." Inside, I'm a tangled mess of nerves and worry, wondering if I'm making the right choice, if I'm getting cold feet, or— My circle of thoughts closes.

Fredrick walks into the room.

All my uncertainty melts away as he breezes down the aisle toward me, looking stunning in his black tux and beaming at me the entire way.

By the time he reaches the end of the aisle, joining us at the altar, I all but collapse in his arms. "You're here."

"I'm here." He holds me, stroking my hair, his touch instantly calming me. "And you're here. And that's all that matters at this moment."

The minister clears his throat. "Mr. Fredrick. It's been a while."

Fredrick looks up, placing the voice with the man it belongs to. "Monsieur, you've come all this way?"

"Oui." He nods my way. "Your beautiful wife requested me."

"I thought you'd want a piece of home here today," I say, hoping he's happy I've taken this liberty. A slow smile eases over his face, allowing me relief. "Is this okay?"

"Yes." He squeezes my hands. "Thanks. Thanks so much."

Everything moves away as if the room and everyone in it melt away behind me; even the minister is only a voice floating between us as we stare into each other's eyes, smiling. We say our vows to one another. We slip thick silver bands onto one another's fingers.

And then he takes my face in his hands, brings me close, and we kiss. This kiss, the first after saying our vows, feels like a seal around our promises. The cheers from our staff, Pearl's clapping hands and gleeful laugh, bring me back to the moment, to the room, the ground now solid beneath my feet.

We eat slabs of vanilla buttercream cake, washing it down with hot tea and coffee, and feed wee bites to our lavender-dressed flower girl, who has no job other than stealing the show.

Tavish, recently recruited for Inverness security, enters the room. All the young, single female staff members turn to watch him walk. The man is gorgeous, lean and pantherlike, owning the air they all breathe as he leans down to whisper in Fredrick's ear.

Fredrick's face changes.

"What is it?" I ask.

"Nothing." He leaves me with a kiss on my cheek. "A work call."

I'm so focused on capturing images of Pearl with my digital camera I don't notice how long he's gone. She's such a wee ham for the camera I barely notice when he returns. Until he says, "Freya. I need to speak with you."

"Okay." Leaving Pearl with Morven, I follow him to the edge of the room.

"I don't know any other way to say this." He puts a hand on the pole he stands next to as if he needs something to lean on for support.

My heart drops to my sparkly wedding shoes. I should have known by how long he was gone that the call would be bad news. "What?"

Finally, he drags his gaze up to meet mine. The look in his eyes makes my stomach drop to my heart-filled shoes. "I've just gotten a call from Glasgow police. The mother has come forward. And her DNA is a match to Pearl's."

Chapter Twenty

F redrick

I'VE NEVER BEEN PROUDER OF MY WIFE'S STRENGTH of spirit than I am when she hands that precious little girl to her mother.

Pearl's grandmother, Cass Owens, works part-time as a secretary at a police borough outside Glasgow. Word of our search reached her over time. Two years ago, her daughter, Leah, who was only nineteen at the time, briefly dated someone much older than her.

A man named Ross Macdonald.

Cass and her husband Joe never took to Ross, even before they found out about his criminal past. During that short time, Leah got pregnant by him.

When the baby was born, Ross demanded custody of the girl. He threatened Leah. Already feeling unsure of her ability to be a mother at such a young age, not to mention becoming a financial burden on her parents, Leah relented.

Her mother, Cass, says that Leah instantly regretted caving to Ross. She cried a lot. She tried to focus on school. And she never stopped pining for her daughter.

A dark-haired baby she had named Ophelia.

Pearl—now we know her name is Ophelia— had grown so close to Freya that she didn't want to go to her mother, Leah. Freya offers the child and mother soothing words. "Don't worry, she'll warm up. She loves everyone."

Leah's young eyes fill with joy and uncertainty as Freya approaches her with Ophelia.

Leah's hands tremble as she reaches to take Ophelia. "I only held her once. At the hospital. She has no idea who I am." Gently, she takes the baby from Freya's arms, her smile beaming, nerves dissolving as she holds her. "Ophelia. Hello. I'm your mam."

Ophelia looks from Leah over to Freya, reaching for her with her little words: "Fre-da. Fre-da."

"It's okay, clever girl." Freya smiles, gesturing to Leah. "This is your mama. Can you say mama?" Her wide blue eyes look from one woman to the other, trying to make sense of this moment.

"Here." Freya slips off the three-strand necklace of pearls she's worn daily since the little girl came into our lives, lovingly placing it around Leah's neck. "Take this. Pearl—I mean, Ophelia...she loves it."

Ophelia takes the familiar beads between her fingers,

relaxing in her mother's arms, and the two quietly study one another's faces.

Leah and her parents spend the day with us, learning Ophelia's routines and likes and dislikes. At one point, Cass looks at Freya and me, saying, "I'd do anything for Leah, and I'll do the same for Ophelia, too." Which makes Freya tear up when Freya's goal is not to cry today.

When the day ends, Freya, a Burnes through and through, can say goodbye without a tear. Me, on the other hand? I am wiping my eyes right to left, pinching the end of my nose, saying, "I must be having allergies."

When the door closes, Freya turns to me, crumpling into my arms. I hold her tightly for a long time, not speaking, only offering comfort. Finally, I say, "I know you're not alright but are you...okay?"

She gazes up at me, a sweet smile on her face. She's striking, sending a pang through my heart. She says, "Whit's fur ye'll no go by ye."

"Meaning?" I ask.

"She belongs with her mam and her kin." Freya shakes her head. "We were only meant to be a stop-by on her way."

Feeling a welling in my chest, I pinch my nose again. "I—I'm glad we could give her a safe place to stay."

"Aye, and I'm grateful we could shield her from her father's death and aid in reuniting her with her family." She wipes away a stray tear. "I know it's right, but it still hurts."

I say, "*Le temps guérit toutes les blessures.*"

"Meaning?" She smiles.

"Time heals all wounds." I wrap my arms tighter around her, returning her head to my chest. I stroke her hair, kissing the top of her head. "It will take time."

"Aye. I know. It helps that Leah has such a sweet spirit. I can't imagine missing the first year and a half of your baby's life."

"Now, her baby is safe in her arms."

"And I made it all day without crying in front of the baby! The last thing I wanted to do was confuse her more."

Now, glassy tears brighten her green gaze, threatening to fall. I want nothing more than to brighten Freya's mood. What can I distract her with? "Let's do something to relax." I name the things she loves. "Wine. Movies. Joyeux."

"Hmm." She pulls back, staring up at me. Her nose crinkles. "No wine. Don't want to get more emotional."

"Ice cream?" I offer. "I could make milkshakes. I have no idea how to do so, but I'm confident I can figure it out."

Her eyes light with mischief. "Now you've got your plough in the ground! Great idea."

"Plough in the ground?" I give her a curious look. "Island saying?"

"Oui!" she confirms. "No one is around this late. They can't stop us from using the kitchen. Let's do it."

We give one another a conspiratorial fist bump.

We change into our matching black silk button-down pajamas. I prefer sleeping in boxers, but happy wife, happy life. She pulls her long hair into the high ponytail I find so sexy, her face bare and clean.

On tiptoe, we sneak off to the kitchen from which we've both been banned.

I stand at the kitchen counter, watching her move gracefully as she pours creamy milk into the blender. I add a generous scoop of rich vanilla ice cream, tasting the cold sweetness on the tip of my finger. Feeling mischievous, I swipe more cream from the carton lid, smearing it over her lips. She playfully kisses me, smearing the ice cream over my cheek in retaliation.

A bowl of freshly washed strawberries is on the counter, tempting me. I grab a handful of berries and drop them into the blender, hoping their sweet flavor mixes with other ingredients.

"Och!" Playfully, she elbows me, adding another scoop of ice cream to the blender. "We agreed on vanilla! Not strawberry."

"Think it's ready?" I ask.

"Let's see!"

Our arms touch as we lean over the blender to see if our milkshake is ready to be blended. A loud noise suddenly jolts me. Freya pushed the button before I secured the lid.

In a split second, creamy white liquid and chunks of fruit fly out of the blender in a chaotic explosion, splattering all over our faces, hair, and clothes, and covering the walls and ceiling.

We both freeze, staring in shock at the mess. Morven's perfect kitchen is destroyed.

"My God, I'm glad Morven's not here right now."

"And just when she was starting to think we might be more than just pretty faces." Laughing, Freya wipes milk from her face. "This is a disaster, not to mention the pasta night failure—"

"Of which we do not speak," I remind her, thinking of the globs of linguini we burned to the bottom of Morven's favorite pan.

"Exactly why we are NOT allowed in the kitchen, husband."

She's so sexy, so utterly sensual, standing there, covered in cream and berries, her long ponytail swishing as she moves toward the towel drawer. "How in the Green Hills of Scotland will we clean up this mess?"

"First," I say, "let's get those messy clothes off you."

I step closer to Freya, my hands reaching for the hem of her soiled black pajama top. I gently lift it up and over her head, revealing her bare skin underneath. She's not wearing a bra, and I stare at the beauty of her breasts, her tight, peaked nipples.

She stands before me, unashamed and unafraid, her confidence making desperate need tighten in my core. I stand there fully dressed and soaked through, wanting her so badly. "You know you're not allowed in the kitchen, naughty girl."

"It was your idea."

"But you pushed the button. What a mess. You'll have to be punished."

With a low growl in my throat, I scoop her up in my arms and carry her to the counter. She gasps softly at the contact, and I can feel her heart pounding against me. Her legs wrap around my waist as I sit her on the cold granite. She shivers at the contact but doesn't pull away from our heated kiss.

"How are you going to punish me?" Freya whispers. Teasing me with sexy naughtiness, she grabs the end of her ponytail, letting her teeth sink into her full bottom lip.

I snag a berry from the bowl, popping it into her mouth. Grinning, she offers me a bite. The taste of strawberries and cream explodes in my mouth, making me even hungrier for her. I kiss her, taking the berry and finishing it for her. Our tongues tangle, tasting one another and the sweet tang of fresh strawberries.

"I'm going to torture you, princess." I dip another strawberry into what's left in the blender, covering it as much as possible with the ice cream. Grabbing the back of her head, I distract her with a deep kiss as I move between her legs. She gasps into the kiss as I tease her entrance with the cold berry, pushing it inside of her.

I lay her down on the island, her back bare on the cold marble, her ass on the edge, her legs over my shoulders. "Lay just like that and take your punishment."

I grab the pitcher of the blender, holding it high. With her hands folded under her head, she stares up wide-eyed. "You wouldn't dare."

Slowly, watching her face every moment, I tilt the pitcher forward. Ice-cold milkshake pours through the air, dripping all over the outer lips of her bare pussy.

She moans from the cold. I go to my knees, pants slipping in the milky mess on the floor. Holding her ass in my hands, I bury my face in her pussy, lapping up sugary cream and the taste of her. I find the strawberry, nipping at its end before pulling it out and feasting on it. I replace the berry with my fingers, stroking her velvet insides as I suck and nibble at her clit.

"Oh God." Her fingers dig into the backs of her thighs. "Oh. God."

With a tight shudder running through her body, she comes fast and hard, back arching over the marble. "Oh MY GOD!"

Satisfied she's pleased, I'm ready to feel her body against me, my cock buried inside her. She lays on the counter, legs hanging down weakly. I stand, rip off my shirt, tear off my pants, and grab her legs.

Before she's fully caught her breath, I pull her from the island, put her on her feet, grab her hips, and flip her around. Gathering cream from the counter, I slide my flat and slippery hand from her lower back up her spine, cupping the back of her neck.

Needing to fuck her, I push her down on the counter. She sucks air in as her bare breasts press against the island. With one hand tangled in Freya's hair and the other holding onto her waist, I guide myself inside of her. We both moan at the feeling of being connected, of friction after so much teasing. Her hands splay, her cheek presses against the marble.

"How hard do you want me to fuck you, princess?" I grab her hips, thrusting deep inside her.

"Harder!" she moans.

"God, you're perfect. "A laugh chokes off in the back of my throat as the first waves of climax start to hit me. My pulse drums in my ear as I hold her hips, pulling her back into me over and over, hard and fast, my pelvis thrusting forward to slam into her each time. Covered in milkshake, my skin grows slick from effort. My fingers find her slippery clit, working it over as I fuck her from behind. "Is this how you like it, hard and fast, my naughty princess?"

"Yes! God. I LOVE the way you fuck." She slaps a palm against the island, gasping as her body tenses. Her shoulders tighten, her neck arching, her head curving back as her pussy locks around me like a clamp. "Fuck, Fredrick! Fuck."

I slap her ass, groaning as I bury my cock inside her, my fingers digging into her hip as I come, hot and flowing, filling her till it spills out of her. I collapse against her back, my chest slick and sticky against her skin. She reaches for the back of my head, stroking my hair. "Damn, you're good at what you do."

"You too, princess." I kiss the back of her neck, savoring the sugar and salt. Gathering her into my arms, I carry her to our massive shower, lathering every inch of her skin. I even shampoo, rinse, condition, and comb her hair for her.

Dressed in robes, our hair damp, we stand in the kitchen doorway, staring at the mess—floors, walls, ceiling all covered in sticky drying cream and chunks of berries.

Sharing a glance, I say, "So this is why they keep us out of here."

"Ready to tackle our biggest challenge yet?"

"No," I say, overwhelmed by the disastrous kitchen. "But Morven will kill us if we don't try."

Chapter Twenty-One

Freya

I don't know if I believe time heals all wounds, but I am pleasantly surprised by how quickly I'm starting to feel better. Sweet Leah sending me daily selfies of her and Ophelia's smiling faces, complete with updates, has helped with the transition, keeping me focused on Ophelia's bright future rather than my own missing her.

As a Burnes does, I throw myself into work. Maybe the saying should be, "Renovations heal all wounds," at least for people like me. I've especially enjoyed the work I've been doing on the Healing Garden.

It's an icy morning, cloudy and overcast. I dress in black leggings, shiny material on the outside, and soft fabric inside to keep my legs warm. I opt for a long pink sweater that covers my bahoochie, to keep my nether region from freezing. After pulling on my tall blue-and-black wool-lined

Overland boots, I grab my long, cream down coat and head outside.

A drizzle starts to fall as I walk toward the stone walls that encapsulate the garden. I should have nabbed a hat on my way out the door. I'm too eager to see the final installment in the garden to turn around and go back to get one.

A turn-off on the path leads to the tall, wooden doors of the garden gates. I've painted them a lovely deep green, installed elegant gold vertical door handles, and hung ivy and cranberry wreaths on them yesterday. An arched sign, lovingly hand-painted by Fiona, sits over the gates.

Welcome to the Healing Garden.

On either side of the cream words Fiona has lovingly painted pink peonies, a flower that represents healing, compassion, and prosperity. These beautiful flowers are known for their healing qualities, often utilized in traditional Chinese medicine.

I'm just about to turn off on the path when I see a figure from around the back side of the East Wing—a very handsome, well-dressed figure wearing a charcoal-gray vest under a long, black wool coat, his dark, damp hair swept back from his forehead.

Och! What's Fredrick doing out here?

Typically avoiding the garden for good reason, he never wanders around this side of the estate. Staying on the path, I hurry to meet him, wanting to keep him as far from the garden gates as possible.

"Och! You! Handsome man." I call out as I get closer, waving with a smile. "What are you doing out here?"

"I could ask you the same." He glances over his shoulder, clearly antsy about whatever he's up to that has him over this way. "It's raining. You should go back into the house."

I narrow my gaze at him, now filled with suspicion. "Och. Ken? Should I go in?"

"Oui. Now."

I'm about to press on, asking why he's so insistent, when I hear a sound come from somewhere behind him. "Was that a...dog bark?"

Hand on his forehead, throwing his head back, he moans. "There is no way to surprise you, wife."

"If you like surprises, don't marry a solicitor." I hear the sound again, close enough to confirm, "It is a dog! I heard it."

I take off jogging, following the path, brushing by him as I go. Over the damp grass, a wee white puppy clumsily frolicks my way. Spotting me, he gives another bark, his shaggy tail standing tall, wagging excitedly, lopsided, crooked to the right.

"Green Hills of Scotland!" My heart bursts in my chest. "Och! A puppy!"

Morven comes wandering up over the hill, blue apron tied around her waist, hollering, "See! Look at all this rain! I warned you: puppy paws bring muddy tracks. You wait till spring."

Hearing Morven's voice, the puppy takes off, zooming to her. Morven's face fully lights from within, beaming with love as she bends at the waist, clapping her hands to call the puppy over. "Come here, ye wee bonnie lass!"

Morven must be in on this. I'm shocked these two could keep me in the dark for this long. "Lass? She's a girl!"

"That she is." Fredrick wraps an arm around my shoulders as we watch Morven scoop up the puppy. "She's a rescue. We've been told she's somewhere between eight and twelve weeks. They think she's Maltese, terrier, and a sprinkling of husky? Morven helped me find the perfect match from the foster agency for our family."

Morven reaches us with the puppy. "There was no question she belonged here at Wee Inverness."

I stare at the bundle of fluff in her arms. "Aww! Rescue! What a wee little warrior. And her name?"

Finally, Morven hands me the dog. "We did the work to find her. The name and Harrods shopping spree are your job." She gives the pup a scratch behind the ear.

The mention of Harrods fills my mind with images of purple collars, sweaters, Burberry dog coats, and wee bows for her fur.

Morven turns, heading to the kitchen, pausing momentarily to turn and eye me. "And don't think I don't know about the milkshake incident! Don't you touch that blender ever again! You two stick to looking pretty outside my kitchen!" Having said her piece, she leaves us, headed back for the kitchen, mumbling about the spring mud coming soon.

Fredrick assures me. "Morven loves the dog, I promise."

"I could see!" I look down at the puppy in my arms. "Morven's all bark and no bite, Merry. I promise."

"Merry?" He smiles.

"This wee beauty was probably born sometime in late December. And I DON'T want Happy feeling displaced." I kiss her wee head. "I christen thee Merry Christmas."

"Perfect," he laughs. "We are a pair, aren't we? Me with my midnight black cat Joyeux Halloween and you with your little white dog, Merry Christmas."

"The very best pair." I stretch up on the toes of my boots, kissing his cheek. "I'm in love with her already."

His voice dips. "I know it doesn't replace Pearl. Nothing can. But I hope the puppy brings you some joy."

"Aye! She does. How can Merry not bring joy!" I joke.

I laugh as the puppy squirms down from my arms, eager to explore more of our estate. Together, we follow her, walking toward the garden. It's lovely, quiet, cold, and overcast.

Finally, I say, "I miss Pearl, but I know she's where she should be." I stare up at him, begging for a kiss. "As am I."

His cold hands envelop my face, giving me the kiss I crave. "I love to hear those words on your pretty lips. You make me so happy, ma chérie."

Merry's headed on the path, off toward the garden gates. There's no time like the present. I look up at him, suddenly shy. "I have something for you as well. Come this way."

Now that the moment of presentation is closing in on me, I begin to worry. Will he love it? Will he hate it? Will it bring him peace and healing, as I thought, or have I done something terrible?

I'm trembling by the time we reach the green garden gates.

"Are you alright, ma chérie? Are you cold? Should we go in?"

I almost wimp out and tell him I'm cold, to take me inside.

Instead, I press on. "It's barren now, but Fiona will come to plant flowers in the spring. Now, I have something in the garden for you. Something I hope brings you healing and peace."

I open the gate. Merry takes off, exploring the best pee spots along the stone wall while I lead Fredrick to the garden's center.

Finally finished and recently delivered, here stands a life-sized bronze statue of his mother, a smile resting on her beautiful face, relaxed wings on her back as she holds a basket in one hand, a flower in her other, gathering ever-lasting blooms from the garden.

I watch his face, hoping I've gotten it right. Tears well in his eyes. My breath hitches in my chest as I wait for his response.

Finally, a slow smile comes over him. "She's free," he says. "She's finally free."

I speak with trembling words. "As you said, it doesn't replace her, nothing can, nothing will, but I hope it brings you some quiet, peaceful moments."

"You have no idea what this means to me." His words warm me; I'm so happy I've finally done something beautiful for him. Wrapping his arms around me, he holds me tight. "Thank you, Freya."

"It was my honor." We stare at the statue quietly, the air filled with emotion.

It's getting cold. I imagine the warm fire in the living room, Happy curled up along the top pillow of the couch. I suggest, "Let's take Merry Christmas to meet Happy Halloween."

"Yes, let's," he agrees.

Taking his hand, I guide us back to the gates. Already a part of the family, Merry follows along, her tail wagging to the right as she prances. I feel so much joy that my wee heart could burst out of my chest.

I give his hand a tight squeeze. Something wells up inside me, demanding to be released. For the first time ever, I tell him, "I love you."

He returns the squeeze, smiling down at me.

He doesn't say it back.

Chapter Twenty-Two

F redrick

She said she loves me. I didn't say it back. She deserves to hear those words from the man she loves. To be told she is loved.

A million times a day.

What if I can never utter those words?

The truth is no one has said them to me since my mother two decades ago. If any woman from my past did feel love for me, I didn't let them get close enough to tell me.

Or maybe they knew if they said those three words—

They'd never see me again.

Freya is safe. No longer in the Kings' inner circle, the Hoax has no use for her. With Erwin's words outlasting his life, everyone knows Freya is loyal to the Kings. Pearl is safe in her mother's arms.

The universe has aligned so that Freya can go out into the world and find her soulmate, and our marriage is new enough to be annulled. She can return to Glasgow and, I don't know—bump into someone at a grocery store, as we've seen in those romance movies from the early 2000s we've watched together.

He'll bump into her, making her drop a watermelon she carries. The fruit will burst, sticky pink all over them. They'll look into one another's eyes and—boom—fall in love. I want that moment for her. I want her to have what I have.

That lightning-strike energy moment I had when I saw her.

She can find someone, marry, and have children. Maybe that friend, Arran, the one behind the boat bar I saw her talking to at her All Hallow's Eve party. The one from the island. He's easygoing, carefree, surely affectionate, and able to tell her he loves her.

They had an easy way with one another—no strain, no tension between them, just a beautiful woman and a man with no damage. And children. She's ready for children. Would I be cursing my children from conception?

Maybe it would be better not to pass on the Frisque name because with it comes my genes—depression and alcoholism from my mother and possible narcissism from my father.

Though selfless, the idea of her with someone else feels so wrong.

We are a pair. We finish one another's sentences. We happily wear matching sweaters, for goodness' sake. Our worlds shrank when we came to Inverness, yet we began to thrive in one another's company.

As for children, my gut clenches at the idea of another man even touching her, much less putting a baby in her.

I've learned that it's not about me, though, and it's time to act on the lesson in the most painful way possible. I need to make the ultimate sacrifice. Set her free. But I've also learned—

I don't make Freya's decisions for her.

I'll do what I must, and Freya will decide.

I sit at the rolltop desk in the living room, pen my note, propose her freedom, and seal the envelope. I leave the letter for her. She will seal our fate.

That night, I sleep in the small guesthouse that used to be MAWR-vein's before I took over, moving her to the larger one. I tossed and turned all night, wondering if I'd done the right thing and if I had, knowing I should have at least done it in person.

When I wake up, I hate myself for being such a coward. I accused Freya of pushing down her emotions, not facing them head-on. Then, I penned my deepest fears and hid. Prickles rise on my skin, sharp and uncomfortable. I rub a hand over the back of my neck. "Why did I leave a letter and run?"

I need to find her. I owe it to her to explain my offer in person. God—what was I thinking? I can't win her back, it's too late, I've made so many mistakes. Still, she deserves to hear the words in the letter straight from me.

There's no way she's still here; surely, she left last night. Still, searching the house first and then traveling to Norse Garden to find her makes sense. I enter the front door. All is silent.

I stand in the foyer momentarily, feeling the house's emptiness without Freya.

I glance up the daunting stairway. The main bedroom will be empty. The bed was unslept in, the covers cold and stark, and pulled taut with MAR-vein's tight tucks. The table that has been set for two every day since her arrival will now be set for one.

I don't bother retrieving the newspaper from the foyer table.

There's no one to read it now.

I hear a bark followed by little paws. Merry gallops across the foyer floor to greet me. "Merry! You're here? I thought you'd go with—" I lean down, scratching her behind her ears. I thought Freya would take the puppy back to Norse Garden with her.

I was clear in the note that Merry belongs to her. Joyeux is mine.

I don't let hope fill my heart as I climb the stairs. She must not have wanted the constant memory of the gift of the dog. I go to open the bedroom door. My pulse thrums in my ears, perspiration dampening my brow.

Am I seeing things?

Freya's seated at our table as she is every morning, the sun streaming in, glittering off her ring, her light hair shining. My chair, across from hers, is empty. I catch a whiff of her floral perfume, confirming she's real.

CAPTIVE MAFIA WIFE

She wears her thin white robe, sipping coffee. Merry trots over to say hello to her.

"This tastes funny. Or is it a smell?" Looking down at the dog—"Merry, did you?" —she sniffs the mug. "Nope. Def the coffee."

Hearing her voice, my heart lunges in my throat. I clear it away. "Didn't you get my note?"

"Och! You scared me!" Startled, she turns to me. "There you are! My God! Where have you been? You haven't even heard the news."

Why is she here? My voice sounds strange. I feel dazed. "What news?"

"The sweetest news ever!" Her face beams as she's barely able to contain her excitement. She pops up out of her seat, prancing over to me. She leans up, kissing my cheek. "Leah reached out. She's giving Ophelia her surname and making a new extract."

The only thing that matters is me and Freya, where we stand. What choice has she made? "That's good. But Freya—"

She keeps talking excitedly. "That's not the best part! Leah's legally changing her name to Ophelia Pearl! Isn't that just darling? She said it was a tribute to us for taking such good care of her daughter." Her hand goes to her heart. "I was so touched and told her you would be as well."

"Of course...yes." What is Freya doing here?

She leaves me, going back to her seat at the table. Pushing the mug of coffee as far from her as possible, she says, "Can you make me a tassie of tea? I can't get it perfect like you do."

"Absolutely." I move without thinking. My mind is so focused on what I said in my note—how I told her she could leave, be free, single, a millionaire, our marriage annulled. How is she still here?

There is only one answer...

She has not read my note. She does not know of my offer. That's why she's still here.

My heart sinks as I remember the words I wrote, my pulse racing in my eardrums as I penned my proposal.

Freya,

You've said the words to me you so deserve to hear. I can't say them. I don't know if I ever can.

You deserve a man who doesn't send a driver to bring you to his home and doesn't keep you captive under the guise of your safety. Did I want to keep you safe? Absolutely. But I brought you here because I was filled with a selfish need to have you since the first moment I saw you.

You deserve so much more. You deserve the world.

Now, I know better. All that matters is that you have everything you want and need. Stay if you wish. Nothing would make me happier.

Or go free.

I'll have the wedding annulled and give you half of everything I own. Take Merry, please, and leave me Joyeux.

Fredrick

Now, she looks up at me expectantly, wanting me to sit, chat, and pour tea.

I slide into the chair. My chair. The one I always sit in. I lift the kettle, filling her favorite delicate teacup only halfway. I tip the milk pitcher, a dot of cream swirling through the tea. My stomach turns, knowing I can't take the coward's way out. This time, I'm forced to tell her in person.

I hand her the tea.

She takes a sip, nodding with approval. "Perfection."

My throat is tight, my words choked. Finally, I say, "My note. Did you read it?"

"That was real?" Her head cocks to the side. Her light brow furrows.

"Yes."

She stares at me until she reads in my eyes that I'm serious. "I laughed when I read it. I thought it was a joke. I thought you were attempting to be more lighthearted." She shrugs. "I mean, I did think you'd taken it a bit far by sleeping somewhere else in the house last night, but I was so tired I passed out after only waiting about five minutes for you to come to bed."

"I meant it."

She puts the teacup down. The glass clinks as the cup rests in the saucer. Her eyes lock with mine for what feels like a full minute.

I don't look away.

"Och! Goodness. You poor thing!" She moves her chair back, coming over to me. "Scootch back."

Obeying, I push my chair back.

She slides into my lap, wrapping her arms around my neck, and says, "Fredrick. Don't you know a thing about islanders?"

I think about the people I know from their small island.

"Hard-working, trustworthy, loyal." I add, "Possibly to a fault."

Perched on my lap, she slips a cool hand on either side of my face, bringing me close enough to smell the scent of her floral perfume. "When we married, I said till death do us part. I meant it. I know you did as well. My brother never would have let you bring me here if you didn't."

"But...I—I can't say those words you need to hear."

Her brow knits. "What words?"

I stare at her, begging her to say them for me because I cannot.

"You mean those three wee words that make the world go round? I love you?" She laughs. The sound is like music to me. "You'd best love me; I went off the pill after—a few weeks ago."

"Wait...what?"

"Seeing you with Ophelia Pearl started my biological clock ticking like crazy! I tossed the contraceptive pills in the trash." She waves a hand through the air. "Truly didn't think ye would mind since you suggested the same months ago."

My heart hammers in my ears. She's ignoring the considerable admission I've just shared with her. That I can't tell her I love her. It's too much for her to process. She's doing that thing where she pushes her emotions down, ignoring them.

I press on. "Freya. Did you hear what I said?"

"Aye, I heard you." To my disbelief, she starts to laugh. "Fredrick. If you loved me any more than you do now, you'd be a psycho stalker." She tilts her head. "You kinda already are psycho for me."

"I'm not capable of love—"

She puts a finger over my lips. "Hush. Don't ever let me hear you say that again."

I put my hand over hers. "But—"

"Haud yer wheesht! And that is NOT a polite way of saying to be quiet, so you'd best heed my words and hush. Now listen to what I have to say." She holds up a hand, ticking things off on her pretty fingers. "Do you trust me?"

"With my life."

Tick. A finger goes down. "Would you make sacrifices for me?"

"I would die a thousand deaths for you, ma chérie," I say.

Another finger is gone. "Am I the first thing you think about when you wake up?"

"Every single morning. And the last thing on my mind when I go to bed." I don't tell her, but often, I dream of her as well.

A third finger is ticked off. "And when you say ma chérie?"

Her arched brows raise. "You're the French one here. Please tell me if you know what that translates to?"

"My darling."

"Exactly." She gives her lawyer nod of confirmation, getting closer to winning her case. "I'm your dear, your darling. Your words, not mine. You have been calling me ma chérie almost since I first arrived. You wouldn't say that if you didn't feel love."

"You sure you don't want…a different kind of man? A different life? You didn't have a choice in coming here…" I don't know what to say.

"I love you. I love our life. I love our story." She kisses me softly and sweetly, a kiss I feel throughout my body. "As long as I can tell you I love you as much as I want, I'll wait forever to hear you say it back."

"You will?" I ask.

"Aye. That's real love." She smiles. "You're protective, reliable, and loyal, even leaving the Kings' inner circle the moment they released me. You're always there for me. If I were to choose a man from a lineup, those are the attributes I would want."

"And you are everything I've always wanted." I touch her face, telling her everything I can. "I'm so sorry I wrote that note. I slept in the guest house and missed one night with you. I should have come to you. I should have told you what I felt—I should have been more courageous."

"What are you talking about? I got a great night of sleep without your snoring."

Of course, my sweet, perfect Freya makes light of this moment. "I don't snore."

"You do, but not to worry." She gives a silly waggle of her brows. "I won't kick you out of my bed. The buttercream icing on the wedding cake is that I find you extremely handsome."

Shocked, relieved, ecstatic, I joyfully joke back, gesturing to the blue-and-green cashmere sweater I wear, one from our collection. "Handsome and well-dressed as well, I hope?"

"Aye." She starts to laugh, but the sound chokes off, and she goes quiet. Has she changed her mind? Her skin pales, turning a funny shade of green, looking, as the Scots say, peely weely. Unwell.

"Och. No." She bends at the waist, erupting her partly digested breakfast all over my chest.

Chapter Twenty-Three

F reya

Merry Christmas is curled by the fire, sleeping cozily on her favorite fuzzy purple bed. Happy Halloween is on the settee next to her, close enough to be friendly but high enough to swat Merry if she gets too rambunctious.

I hear Morven passing by in the hall, singing quietly to herself as she dusts.

I rock back and forth on my glider, staring at the silver-framed photos that line the mantle. There's one from our wedding, Fredrick and me, smiling wide. The latest photo of wee Miss Ophelia Pearl settled and safe in her mother's arms, with the lovely English countryside of her grandparents' cottage in the background. The one I took of Fredrick in his sweater when he first gave me the camera.

The last frost will come soon. Callum and Fiona will visit to welcome spring. Fiona will show me how to plant jasmine vines, blooming shrubs, peonies, and other flowers in the Healing Garden.

Callum and Fredrick will visit with one another, no longer planning on waging wars. Instead, they will battle one another on the golf course; Fredrick will wear his pink-and-green plaid sweater from our collection for the game.

Not interested in traveling to Glasgow, and neither of us drinking whisky any longer, Fredrick has sold the distillery and his other businesses to the Kings, the considerable profits going straight into the bank.

My life is now in Inverness, and my whole world fits inside this cozy, well-decorated living room. I am no longer anyone's captive or target. No longer a part of the Kings. Not a practicing solicitor. I'm just a wife, loved and cherished. I feel free. I feel complete. The girls from the firm will be here for my baby shower in a few weeks. Soon, I'll be a mother, and the precious baby in my belly will join our happy family.

After my husband's trauma and my feeling the pain of having a child torn away from us, for now, we've made a career compromise.

We'll both be stay-at-home parents.

We're fortunate enough to afford the time together. Neither of us wants to miss a moment of this baby's life. And I don't want to miss a single day with my husband.

Merry and Happy lift their heads, seeing who's entering the room. Happy gives a lazy yawn. Merry, too tired, drops her head back down on her paws.

I smile at my husband as he walks in, holding a cup of tea. "Hello there, handsome." The scent of peppermint reaches me. Morven sent it to settle my stomach. I take the cup he hands me. "Thank you."

"Of course, my love." He kisses my head before dropping to a knee beside me. His hand goes to my belly, gently rubbing circles. "And how is this little one today?"

I smile. "Sleeping soundly. Hasn't moved in an hour or so. Only two more months before she joins us in person. I can't wait."

"I'm dying to meet our little girl, but I must admit…If I could keep her safe in your belly forever, would I?"

"I know you would!" I laugh. "Wait till you hold her the first time. You'll change your mind."

"You know I'm a worrier, though. That I'll be overprotective." Standing, he runs his hand through his hair. "I'm going to drive her crazy."

"No," I correct. "She will be head over heels for you just as Pearl and I are." I take his hand, bringing it back to my belly. "This baby will love you with her whole heart."

His eyes find mine. "Just as I adore you both with my whole heart."

"Exactly," I say, my breath catching in my throat.

He's so close…will he finally be able to say the words I long to hear?

"Ma chérie." He leans in, kissing me sweetly before pulling back so our eyes can meet. That energy between us from the beginning pulses as we stare at one another. With warmth, he says, "My lovely lass of Inverness. I love you. I love you so very much. And I love our baby."

I knew he was capable of love, and I knew he would say the words one day. I'm so filled with joy I could burst. "I love you, too."

Our baby chooses this moment to wake up, giving a sharp movement against my belly where Fredrick's hand still rests.

"I felt her move!" he laughs. His eyes glitter with happiness as he asks, "Do you think she was giving me a fist bump for finally saying the words or kicking me for taking too long?"

"Neither." I put my hand over his. "That was your wee Freida saying, I love you, too."

The only tears in the eyes of this Inverness lass are tears of joy when he kisses me softly and says, "I love you," one more time.

"I love the sound of those words coming from you," I say, wiping away a tear. "Say them again."

And my dear Fredrick, so strong, so caring, so void of love before *he* and *I* became *we* and *us*... repeats the precious words.

"I love you," he says. "Forever and ever."

The End... but the story isn't over!

BONUS EPILOGUE 16 YEARS LATER...

Ophelia

I stare into the stranger's dark eyes. "You want me to pay my mother's debts?"

"I have more money than god." He man gives me a wicked grin. "The debt she owes me is one the head of a two-sided coin."

"And tails?"

He grabs me, pulling me close. His breath is hot against my ear. His voice is heat and danger. "I'll take you to make her suffer."

"That's cruel." My voice is a weak whisper. His scent, muscular frame, and size overwhelm my senses as he becomes a dangerous cocoon around me.

His heated words continue. "It's a cold, cruel world, little girl. The sooner you figure that out, the easier it will be to join my world."

He has yet to learn how early I was introduced to the concept. I shake my head. "You know nothing about me."

"I know you're a beautiful virgin, and your mother owes me a hell of a lot of money. And, she must pay back the greatest debt of all."

"Being?"

"Respect," he growls. "She disrespected me. She needs to learn; if you disrespect a man of the Bachman Brotherhood, you pay very dear consequences."

KEEP READING...

CAPTIVE MAFIA WIFE

BRAND NEW SERIES featuring Ophelia and her family. Here's a tease for you, lovely reader. Just a taste to *wet* your appetite.

xoxoShanna

Vow of Vengeance: A Dark Mafia Revenge Marriage Romance is from the new series, *Bachman Brotherhood Revenge Romance.*

I'm held captive on a lavish estate. The mafioso demands I marry him... And give him my V-card.

This is revenge for what my mother did.
Millions of dollars that he plans to take out on my virgin body.
Seductive day by day. Punishing hour by hour.

Forever, til' death do us part.

I have to fight him, but he's too powerful.
His force terrifies me. His rare tenderness tempts me.
Will I become his obedient wife, or will I fight for freedom?

READ NOW!

Power, Family Secrets, BDSM

This dark mafia steamy series is in the same world as Ophelia's story!

VOW TO THE KING is STILL my most popular book to date. When it first released, it broke #1 on THREE New Release charts and was an instant bestseller. It'a little dark, gritty, and intense. It's the first in a completed series of stand-alones if you'd like to give it a try.

A desperate young virgin finds her life forever changed when she runs into the dangerous hands of a mafia man who traps her in this steamy mafia romance novel.

Psst...wanna know a secret? The last book in the Twisted Mafia Kings Series, titled Captive Mafia Wife, will circle back to this book, Vow to the King.

xoxoShanna

Also by Shanna Handel

I'd love for you to join my newsletter, please~
www.shannahandelromance.com/newsletter
(I share adorable pet photos)

Bachman Brotherhood Revenge Romance Series
Vow of Vengeance: A Dark Mafia Revenge Marriage

Twisted Mafia Kings Series

New BILLIONAIRE ROMANCE Series

BACHMAN BROTHERHOOD LEGACY

DARK MAFIA ROMANCE SERIES

Vow to the King: A Dark Mafia Romance

Mafia Fire: A Dark Mafia Romance

Mafia Beast: A Dark Mafia Romance

Mafia Captor: A Dark Mafia Romance

Mafia Savior: A Dark Mafia Romance

DARK DADDY DUET

Stalk Me Gently: Daddy's Obsession Book 1
Praise Me Sweetly: Daddy's Obsession Book 2

Billionaire Romance Series

For fans of Fifty Shades of Grey

Beauties&Billionaires Billionaire Romance Series

DARK ROYALS: DARK MAFIA ARRANGED MARRIAGE ROMANCE SERIES

Book ONE

DARK CROWN

Book TWO

DARK THRONE

Book THREE

DARK KINGDOM

Book FOUR

DARK FOREST

Book FIVE

DARK CASTLE

My first series!

Bronson: A Mafia Billionaire Romance

I like nice things, but this time I've stolen from the wrong man.

He caught me red-handed, but he didn't call the police.

He's the kind of man who settles his own scores.

Buy on Amazon

Carter: A Mafia Billionaire Romance

She is mine. It's time she learned what that means.

In my world, a man keeps his woman in line.

She is used to doing as she pleases.

That is about to change...

Buy on Amazon

Rockland: A Mafia Billionaire Romance

The code of the family makes her mine to protect, but I will make her mine in every way.

I moved across the world to escape my need for her.

Then my brother's death left her a widow.

I gave her time to grieve, but now I will take what is mine.

Buy on Amazon

Virgin: A Mafia Billionaire Romance

Yesterday I'd never been kissed. Today every inch of me belongs to him.

I didn't ask for a guardian, but it wasn't up to me.

I disobeyed him, just to see what he would do.

Then I found out what happens to bad little girls.

Buy on Amazon

Love Daddy Dom Romance?

Bachman Daddies: A Mafia Billionaire Romance Series

Click Here for Book 1- Daddy

Click Here for Book 2- Say Daddy

Book 3- Daddies: A MFM Ménage Romance

Book 4: Her Mafia Daddies MFM Ménage Romance

Vegas Daddies with Jane Henry

Click here for Be My Babygirl

Click here for Always My Babygirl

Click here for Forever My Babygirl

Love Cowboy Romance?

Shanna Handel's Cowboy Dom Ranch Rules Series

Printed in Great Britain
by Amazon